The lid on the dark coffin was open and we could see something move. Ashley screamed right in my ear. . . .

"Oh, for crying out loud, Ashley! You want to make me deaf or something?" I didn't want to admit I was as scared as screaming Ashley.

I was almost at the coffin—Ashley had stayed behind—when the low moaning began. . . . Okay—enough was enough.

"Come on, Ashley," I said, practically falling over myself. "Let's get out of here."

But Ashley wasn't moving. Her mouth was wide open, and she was pointing at something behind me. I figured she was scared silly. . . .

Books by M. M. Ragz

Eyeballs for Breakfast
Eyeballs for Lunch
Sewer Soup
Stiff Competition

Available from MINSTREL Books

STIFF
COMPETITION

M. M. RAGZ

A
MINSTREL®
BOOK

PUBLISHED BY POCKET BOOKS

New York   London   Toronto   Sydney   Tokyo   Singapore

A MINSTREL PAPERBACK *ORIGINAL*

A Minstrel Book published by
POCKET BOOKS, a division of Simon & Schuster
1230 Avenue of the Americas, New York, NY 10020

Copyright © 1991 by Margaret M. Ragozzino
Cover artwork copyright © 1991 by Bob Tanenbaum

ISBN: 0-671-72522-X

First Minstrel Books printing February 1991

10 9 8 7 6 5 4 3

A MINSTREL BOOK and colophon are registered trademarks of Simon & Schuster

Printed in the U.S.A.

Dedicated to my parents
Henry and Erna Muhlmeister
with love

Chapter

ONE

I step up to the foul line. The ref hands me the basketball. From the stands I hear the crowd of ten thousand chanting my name: MUR-PHY, MUR-PHY. I am cool under pressure. I am the youngest member of the U.S. Olympic team. I am small but great. If I make this shot, the U.S. will win the gold medal.

I dig my toes deep into my sneakers. I bounce the ball twice. My fingers feel along the seams as I concentrate on the basket. The chanting becomes a deafening roar—then silence as I release my shot. It arcs high. I watch the ball—as if in slow motion—fall toward the hoop. The shot is . . .

Blocked! By my mother, who walked into the family room, reached up, and grabbed the Nerf ball just before it dropped into the homemade hoop I had taped onto the fireplace.

"Murphy," she said, squeezing the ball in her fist, "I told you this is *not* a gym. And take that contraption off the fireplace before something gets ruined."

"But Mom, Dad told me to practice. I'm trying out for the Senior League this year. The kids in that league are all in middle school. This is the first year that they're taking a couple of players from Junior League. I think I could make it."

She looked at me and shook her head. "I don't see why you can't play in the Junior League for another year. You're a star player. Why be a little fish in a big pond? Why do you want to grow up so fast?"

"Because I'm ready. And Dad thinks I can make it. And I'm tired of the Junior League. And I need a new challenge."

I dropped to the floor and started doing knuckle pushups. I wanted to be like my dad, who had been a great athlete and was now the head basketball coach at Westford High School. I had been going to his practices and games since I was old enough to walk. Basketball was in my blood. Dad said so.

Mom stood over me as I grunted my way through the twentieth pushup. "You're being ridiculous. All this groaning and sweating and working out. You should be out playing."

"You don't understand. They're only going to choose one Junior League player for each team. There are twelve teams. Every kid in Junior League who gets recommended by his coach will be trying out, and I want to make sure I get one of those twelve spots."

I flipped over on my back, picked up a regulation basketball, and started tossing it up in the air and catching it. It was a conditioning drill Dad used with his team.

Mom snatched the ball in midair. "Enough, Murphy. Set the table. It's almost time for dinner."

"Ma," I protested as I started a set of sit-ups, "tell Tony to set the table. Or Kenny. I'm in training. Just because I'm the youngest doesn't mean I should get stuck with all the slave labor around here."

She wouldn't listen. "Tony's studying for a psychology exam and Kenny works all day. You're not doing anything important right now. So, young man, you set the table."

"Nothing important? Are you trying to say basketball's not important?" But I knew there was no point arguing with her. My two older brothers seemed to get away with murder. Kenny was twenty-four and working full-time. Tony was nineteen and going to Westford Community College.

"When are those guys moving out?"

Mom just smiled and rubbed my head. "They can live here as long as they want to. Dad loves having all his boys at home."

I started banging plates and silverware on the table, dreaming about how I would be the star of a Senior League team. Suddenly the phone rang. "I'll get it," I yelled, figuring it would be my best friend Peter Patterson. He'd been calling a lot to talk about tryouts. Like me, he was hoping for one of the twelve Senior League positions.

"Hello?" It was for me, all right, but it was Ashley Douglas, number-one pest who had recently appointed herself my number-one friend. She spent a lot of time telling everyone she was my girlfriend. I wasted a lot of time telling everyone she wasn't.

3

"Hi, Murphy. You said you'd call."

"No, I didn't. I never said that!"

"Yes, you did. After school, when I wanted to give you a ride home, you said, 'Don't call me, I'll call you'. Remember?"

"It was meant as a joke, Ashley. I thought you were smart enough to get the message."

"I did. That's why I'm calling. To remind you that you said you'd call."

That Ashley. Whenever she started playing stupid—watch out.

"So what do you want?" No sense wasting words. With Ashley it was always best to get right to the point.

"Want to go downtown to the library tomorrow after school?"

"What for?"

"To study."

"With you?"

"Of course with me."

"Like I said—what for?"

"Because we're the two smartest kids in class. And when we put our two minds together, it's like electricity."

"Yeah—painful," I muttered.

"What?"

"I said that's really plain to see. Listen, I'd like to. Really. But I have to go somewhere with my dad tomorrow. He said it would take all afternoon." I didn't want to lie, but Ashley never took a straight 'no' for an answer. "Maybe some other time."

"Well, if you're sure you're busy—with your dad, I mean—I could meet you after. My mom's dropping me off at the library."

"Like I said, I just can't, Ashley. Mom's calling me to finish the table. Gotta go."

"Call me sometime, Murphy?"

"Don't call me, I'll call . . ." I caught myself. That smart line had gotten me into this call. "Yeah, sure. I'll call." She was saying something, but I pretended not to hear and hung up fast.

Mom was standing next to me. "What was that all about?"

"It's a long story. Could you give me a ride downtown tomorrow after school? Peter and I want to go to the YMCA, but we need a ride. We want to get in some practice before tryouts. Greg and Michael are coming with us. They're not trying out, but they're going to help us practice. We'll get a ride home with Peter's dad."

"I guess so. As long as you get your homework done. That's one thing I know comes before basketball."

"Right, Mom."

"Now go call your brothers."

As Mom dished out the spaghetti and meatballs at dinner, Dad piled a big bunch of salad onto my plate. "Have you been practicing, Murphy?" he asked. "I want to see you in top form for the tryouts. When do they start?"

"Day after tomorrow," I answered, reaching for the bread and butter.

Dad took the butter from me. "Have to watch your

fats. The carbohydrates are okay, but the fat you eat is the fat you wear. And eat plenty of salad.''

Tony, who sat next to me, reached over my plate, grabbed the butter dish, and wiggled it under my nose before he plopped it down next to him. He spread a big slab of bread thick with butter.

Dad just ignored him. "Tryouts, Murphy. I'll come. Maybe I'll make a call—make sure you make it.''

"No way. I'll make it on my own. And I'll go to tryouts alone. I don't want anyone thinking you helped me. Promise you won't make any calls for me, okay?''

Ken, who had already vacuumed up two dishes of spaghetti and was reaching for a third, said, "Think you can make it, big guy? That's a pretty tough league. I played in it a few years ago.''

"Sure I can make it. You didn't make it until you were in seventh grade. I'm not that old, and I can outshoot you now.''

It was true. I was an amazing shooter, and the whole family knew it. It was something Dad was especially proud of. "You've got my genes, Murphy," he said. "When you concentrate, you can't miss.''

"I know, Dad. Just like you taught me. I put my mind into the ball, and I can make it drop through every time.''

Tony picked his head up from his plate and asked, "What about when you miss, Murphy? What's your excuse then?''

"I only miss when something distracts me. Like your ugly face, for example.''

Dad cleared his throat. "*Nothing* should distract you,

6

Murphy. A top shooter can shut out all distractions. We'll work on it. As a matter of fact, if tryouts start the day after tomorrow, we'd better start practicing. Get a ball and meet me in the driveway. I'll change into my workout clothes.''

He left without finishing his spaghetti. That's when I realized how badly he wanted me to make a Senior League team.

Chapter

TWO

I was getting ready to leave for school the next morning when Dad stopped me.

"Murphy, where are you going with that ball? That's Westford's championship ball from last year."

"I know. And I'll be really careful with it. I told Peter I'd bring a good-luck basketball for us to use at the Y this afternoon. Can I use it, Dad? Just this once? It'll help us be serious about practicing. And Senior League tryouts start tomorrow. Please?"

He looked doubtful. "If anything happens to that ball, I'm going to be very upset. I don't think you should take it to school. Someone might walk off with it."

"Mom's giving us a ride downtown. I'll leave it in the car and just use it after school. It means a lot to me and the guys. Please?"

He took a deep breath, thought for a second, and said, "I like your determination to practice. If you're absolutely sure nothing will happen to it . . ."

"Absolutely. Honest. You're a great dad. I love you."

"Me, too. Just don't lose that ball, son." Whenever Dad called me son, I knew he meant business. But what could possibly happen to a basketball?

After school Mom dropped the four of us downtown about two blocks from the YMCA, in front of the Snack Shack. We figured we needed a little energy before we got to our workout.

"Peter's dad will pick us up at five. I'll be home for dinner." I grabbed Dad's prize basketball and we all thanked her for the ride.

While we ate our fries, we talked about how great it would be to be on a Senior League team.

"That's really big time," said Greg. "Think you and Peter have a chance?"

"Sure we do," I said. "Especially since you and Michael came along to help us practice. Come on. Let's go."

As we walked the first block toward the YMCA, we passed the ball back and forth. Peter caught the ball and was about to pass it to me, but he stopped short.

"What's the matter?" I asked.

"Isn't that Ashley and some of the girls?" he asked.

"Where?"

"Down there." He pointed. Sure enough, there was Ashley with Steffie Whiffet and Jennifer Fisher, about a block ahead of us, walking in our direction.

"Oh no," I groaned. "I'm dead for sure. I told her I was going somewhere with Dad. She'll never stop pestering me now. And if she sees us, we'll *never* get rid of her."

"I don't think they saw us," said Michael. "Come on. Let's cut down this alley."

We ran down one alley, dashed down another, cut through a parking lot, and ended up on a narrow street I had never seen before. When we stopped running, we were all panting and puffing. I caught my breath and said, "Thanks, guys. I hate to be caught in a lie. Especially by someone like Ashley!"

"What are friends for?" said Peter.

Greg was facing us but was looking wide-eyed past us across the street. We turned to see what he was staring at.

He pointed toward a huge old house that sat on a small hill. "Wow! That's got to be the spookiest-looking house I've ever seen."

"It looks empty," Michael said.

"It is. It has a 'for sale' sign in front of it. Come on, let's get a closer look. I've never seen a real haunted house before," Peter said.

I didn't want to go exploring such a creepy place, but I didn't have much choice. Peter led the way, followed by Michael and Greg. I trailed behind, carrying the basketball.

We stood at the bottom of a long stone staircase that led to the front door. "Look, there's a sign hidden behind those bushes," Greg said as he pulled some branches aside and read the faded old wooden sign: "The Bedford Funeral Home." He jumped back.

"I told you the place was haunted," Peter said. "Let's go around back."

Even though it was a sunny day, the house seemed to

stand in shadow. Paint was peeling, shutters were hanging, and a few windows were broken. It made me feel cold.

Peter was still in the lead, but we kept walking slower, and as we got to the back, we were practically holding our breath. There were steps up to the back door, too, and a wide, rickety back porch.

"Want to go up and look around?" asked Peter.

"Not especially," said Michael. "This place gives me the shivers. Let's go."

I thought that was a good idea, but Peter said, "Not yet. Look. There's a broken cellar window. Let's look in, at least."

We crouched around the window. It was pretty dark down there, but we could see cabinets, shelves, and some kind of a big metal table bolted down in the middle of the room.

"Looks like an operating room," said Greg.

"Yeah. Or a laboratory. Maybe they did experiments on the bodies down there," said Peter. "Like Frankenstein."

"Maybe it's haunted."

"Oh, boy, I hope so," said Peter. He was my very best friend, but he sure had a weird streak.

"Look over in that corner. Isn't that a body bag? Maybe it's still occupied," he said, starting to chuckle like he was Dracula or something.

We were staring hard into that window and having a great time scaring each other.

Suddenly something that felt like a skeleton's finger brushed the back of my neck. One of the guys was

11

trying to scare me, probably Peter, but I didn't want to turn around. "Cut it out," I said. As I did, he looked at me and I noticed that his hands and everyone else's were in front of us. I felt the scratchy finger on my neck. Then it poked me in the back.

Suddenly we all heard a low moaning sound. We were all huddled down close together, and Greg whispered, "What was that?"

"Something's touching my neck," I said.

"Something's on my back," said Michael, his voice squeaking.

Even Peter looked pale.

We turned around slowly to face the unknown when something came screaming at us. Ashley! With Steffie and Jennifer right behind. Ashley was carrying a long dead branch.

The four of us bumped into each other trying to get up. In the confusion the basketball was knocked out of my hands.

"Ashley, what are you trying to do? Scare us to death?" I asked.

"It would serve you right after lying to me. You said you had to do something with your father."

"I didn't exactly lie. Basketball tryouts start tomorrow, and . . . and . . ." I was stuck.

Greg picked up where I had stopped. "And Murphy's father is putting a lot of pressure on him to make a team, and . . . and . . ."

Peter was next. "And so is my dad. So we promised them that we'd practice all afternoon so we'd get on a team, and . . . and . . ."

"And that's what friends are for," finished Michael. "To help each other out."

Ashley looked at each of us. She didn't know what to say for once.

She turned to leave, and we were all about to slap each other high fives when she turned back and said, "Oh, yeah? Then if you're going to practice basketball, where's your basketball?"

"It's right here," I said, turning around to get the ball. "Right over . . ." I started to look around frantically. "Hey, guys, where's the ball?"

"You had it," said Michael. "You were holding it when we were looking in that cellar window."

Peter ran back to where we had all been crouching. "It's not here."

"We've got to find that ball," I said. "My dad'll kill me! It must have rolled somewhere."

The four of us scattered to look around.

Steffie and Ashley walked over to the window we had been looking in. "There it is," said Steffie. "I see it."

I breathed a sigh of relief. "Where?"

"In there. It must have rolled through this broken window."

Peter, Greg, Michael, and I squeezed together with Ashley and Steffie to peer through the window.

"See it?" asked Steffie, pointing.

"Yup," said Greg. "Right next to the body bag."

"How are we going to get it?" I asked, feeling a little sick.

"What do you mean *we*?" asked Michael. "You mean how are *you* going to get it."

"Me? Me? I didn't want to come here in the first place. And if it hadn't been for Ashley and her dumb jokes—"

"Don't look at me," Ashley said, putting her hands on her hips. "I'm not going into any spooky old cellar— especially not for a silly old basketball."

"It's not silly. It's my father's championship ball."

We all walked away from the window and sat on the grass. "We could try to get in," said Greg.

"Bad idea," said Michael. "Even if it's not haunted, I for one am not going to wander around a funeral home."

We all agreed and got quiet again. Then Steffie said, "I used to know the family who lived here. Or at least my father did."

"What do you mean 'family'?" Michael asked.

"Yeah. It's a funeral home," said Greg. "Not a *home* home. Don't be dumb, Steffie."

"I'm not being dumb. You are. The man who owned this place lived here with his whole family. They moved about a year ago."

"That's weird," said Greg.

"That's sick," said Michael. "Living in a funeral home is the sickest thing I ever heard of."

"That's neat," Peter said. "Think they slept in coffins?" He started walking around all monster-stiff-legged, making strange sounds and putting stiff fingers around everyone's throats.

Ashley screamed and giggled and started chasing him. Greg ran after Ashley, and pretty soon everyone was laughing and playing monster. Except me.

14

I didn't know what I'd say to Dad. "It's getting late. Let's go."

They all came over, and we were about to leave when Greg said, "Hey, where's Peter?"

Everyone looked around.

"I don't know," said Ashley. "He was here a minute ago."

"Well, he's not here now." Losing a basketball was one thing; losing a good friend was a completely different story. We started running around yelling his name.

Suddenly we heard a voice. "Hey, guys, you should see this. It's neat." Peter! But we couldn't figure out where he was.

"Hey," he hollered again, "I'm down here. Want to come down and look around?" His voice was coming from the basement of the funeral home. I ran over to the window. There was Peter, my basketball in his hand, grinning up at me.

"Peter, how'd you get down there? Come out of there."

"I found a door around the side that was open. It led to the basement. I couldn't let you lose your basketball, could I?"

"Thanks, Peter. Now hurry up and get out of there, okay?"

He disappeared through a door and appeared around the side of the house. I was relieved to see him.

As he threw the ball to me he said, "It's a neat old place. Maybe someday you'll see what I mean."

"You're crazy," I said. "A funeral home is the last place you'll ever see me."

Everybody started to laugh, but I didn't see anything funny.

Chapter

THREE

The next afternoon almost fifty Junior Leaguers from all over town had come to tryouts at the Westford Middle School gym. We all knew there were only twelve openings in the Senior Division, and we all thought we were good enough to make it.

"What do you think, Peter?" I asked. "Look at all these kids. Think we have a chance?"

"*You* have a great chance, Murphy. Your dad's got pull. He's on the board of directors of the league or something, isn't he? That's what my dad says."

"Let me tell you something. If I make the Senior League, I make it by myself. Dad won't help me."

"Sure. Whatever you say." Peter was my best friend, but I guess these tryouts had nothing to do with friendship.

The coach who was running tryouts blew his whistle. "You're each wearing a number. The coaches from the Senior League will be walking around the gym and will be judging you only by the numbers you're wearing."

Peter was standing next to me on the sideline. "So that's who those guys are. Senior League coaches."

Each of those coaches wore a trim and shiny sweatsuit; each carried a clipboard; each wore a hat with his team name on it. They reminded me of my father—all business when it came to basketball. I was getting a little nervous.

Because there were no basketball teams in elementary or middle school in Westford, the Junior and Senior Leagues had been set up instead. The teams were sponsored by local businesses who bought uniforms and trophies, paid for officials, and sponsored banquets at the end of the season.

The coach continued to explain. "All of you will try out today and tomorrow after school. The top twenty-five players will have a final tryout on Saturday. The players who make Senior League will be chosen from that group. Good luck to all of you."

For the first two days of tryouts—Thursday and Friday after school—we were put into groups with a Junior League coach. They were nice guys who smiled a lot and tried to give us confidence. Even when a kid missed a layup or threw an airball they'd say something nice like "Good try" and pat the kid on the back.

All the while the Senior League coaches prowled around the gym, never smiling, never even nodding, just stopping to watch and make notes.

We went through shooting drills—layups, jump shots, foul shots. Peter was in my group, and we both did pretty well. I blew a couple of layups that rolled around the rim and bounced off, but my form was good. When

17

it came to the foul shots, I missed only once. I had hit five in a row and then noticed a Senior League coach watching. When I tried to show off, the ball hit the front of the rim and bounced off. I saw him write something down and move on. I didn't know if that was a good sign or not.

For the rest of the tryout time, the groups scrimmaged against each other. Every time I got in I tried to be a team player, like I heard my father tell his ballplayers. A team player doesn't hog the ball—when he gets it he looks up and tries to pass to an open man.

A lot of kids didn't do that. As soon as they got the ball they would "showboat"—dribble the length of the court and go for the shot.

At the end of Friday's tryouts, the coach blew his whistle, waited for us to settle down, and said, "Okay, guys. Listen up. Sit on the floor here in front of me."

Dirty and sweaty and tired, Peter and I sat on the floor, our hearts pounding. I shook my fist. "Good luck, Peter."

Peter crossed as many fingers as he could. "Here's for both of us making it."

The whistle blew again, and we could hear nothing but breathing as all of us waited for the names to be read.

"Before I read the names," he said, "I have to congratulate all of you on a great job. The following twenty-five athletes are to report to tryouts tomorrow."

I held my breath and kept my eyes on a speck of dirt

on the floor as he slowly read through the list. Just when I lost all hope of making the cut I heard him say, "Murphy Darinzo." And then, "Peter Patterson."

I blew out a deep breath of relief. I looked over at Peter, and we both broke into big grins. We just kept looking at each other, grinning stupidly, until he said, "Slap me five, Murphy," and we slapped each other high fives until my hands hurt.

Chapter

FOUR

Murphy, you'd better let me come with you." Dad and I were having an early Saturday morning breakfast together before I left for the final round of tryouts.

"I don't think so. It wouldn't be right. Too many people know you. I don't want anyone saying I didn't make it on my own. Peter and his dad are giving me a ride."

When we got to the gym, I wondered if I had made the right decision about Dad. There were twenty-five kids, and almost as many mothers and fathers. The Senior League coaches were already there, and quite a few parents were near them, talking.

Some boys were on the court with basketballs they had brought along, dribbling through their legs and behind their backs.

I slipped off my sweats and walked toward a kid I knew from school who was dribbling around by himself in the middle of the court. "Hey, Scott. Over here. Can I see the ball?" I put my hands out to catch the ball.

He looked up at me, stopped dribbling, and held the ball out. "Sure. See it?" Then he turned his back on me and started dribbling again.

"Thanks, Scott. You're a real pal," I said as I walked up in front of him and got into a defensive position. As he tried to dribble past me, I slapped the ball away. He said something nasty under his breath as he chased the ball, then went to the other side of the gym to continue his fancy dribbling alone.

We had the same numbers we'd had for the last two days. A Senior League coach stood at midcourt, blew a whistle to get our attention, and said, "Time to get this show on the road. Tryouts today are all playing time. Each of you is assigned a team. Two teams will play at a time."

"Wow," whispered Peter. "This is big time. Not like the Junior League tryouts we had a couple of years ago, huh? We're going to have to be great to make a team."

"I guess so," I answered. But my mind was on Peter's father, who was standing near a coach, talking his ear off. Maybe I should have listened to Dad.

"What's your team number, Murphy?"

"Two."

"I'm on four. See you on the court." He shook out his arms and walked away. He looked back over his shoulder and called, "And remember: friends no matter what."

The games were rough. And it didn't take us long to realize that the refs—two of the Senior League coaches—weren't going to call many fouls. And since we were all trying to show our best skills, it was more like ten individuals fighting to score rather than two teams playing.

21

I played hard, and I got elbowed, body-blocked, and dumped on my seat more than once, and not always by the other team.

When I sat with my team on the sidelines I watched closely. The only sounds were sneakers squealing against the floor, kids grunting when they got hit or went for a shot, and the thud-thud of the dribbled ball echoing off the gym walls. No one cheered for anyone; no one slapped five when somebody else scored.

It was a rough and lonely tryout, but my father's voice bounced through my brain: "Q.C., Murphy. Quiet confidence. Just play your game. No one wants a show-off. Be a team player."

"I hope you're right, Dad," I thought as I watched a kid dribble behind his back, ignore an open man, and drive in for a ferocious layup.

Every so often a coach would blow his whistle and call a number to the foul line. "Game situation," he'd say. "Your team is down by one point, three seconds on the clock. It's a one-and-one. Make the first foul shot, you tie the game and maybe win with your second shot—team champ. Miss the shot, and your team loses the game, and you're team chump." Talk about pressure. A lot of kids didn't make the shots.

When we got down to our last time on the court, play was doubly rough. I had two chances to drive in for a layup but chose to pass off to an open teammate under the basket instead. I dived a couple of times for a loose ball, ignoring the pain that ripped over my elbows and knees from floor burns.

I didn't have a shot at the foul line until the end of play when a coach blew his whistle. "Okay, number twenty-one," he said. "Your team wins or loses on this play. Go."

I stood at the foul line. It took me three deep breaths and three deliberate bounces of the ball to make everything around me fade away. There was nothing in that gym except me, the ball, and the hoop. I made both shots.

The final whistle blew and we sat in a semicircle around the coach. "If you make a team," he said, "you'll get a call between four and five o'clock this afternoon. And for those of you who don't make it, feel good anyway because you'll definitely be the star players on your Junior League teams."

Peter and I waited around while Mr. Patterson had a few last words with a coach. It looked to me like he was working extra hard to make sure Peter had a very good chance.

FIVE

I was quiet on the ride home, but Peter and his dad didn't seem to notice—they were too busy talking about Peter's tryout and how well he had done. I might have been wrong, but it sounded like they were making big-time plans for Peter.

Mom and Dad were waiting for me when I got home.

"Well?" Dad asked. "How did it go?"

Mom just watched as I pulled off my sweatshirt. My shaggy blond hair was matted to my head with dried sweat. One elbow was scraped red, and the other had started bleeding as a new scab was brushed by the sweatshirt.

"Oh, my gosh, look at you," Mom said. "What happened? Were you in a fight? You said basketball tryouts, not tackle football."

I looked past her at Dad, who was smiling. "I don't even have to ask," he said. "You did your best. When will you find out?"

"The coach said the kids who make it will get a call

today between four and five.'' Dad and I both looked at the clock—12:50. It was going to be a long three hours and ten minutes.

By four o'clock I was a wreck. Mom was shopping, Ken and Tony were out, and Dad said he was going for a jog—he always worked out when he was nervous—so I was alone to watch the minutes tick by. I turned on the TV and tried to concentrate on an old black-and-white Laurel and Hardy movie, but my eyes kept drifting over to the clock.

At 4:15 I picked up the phone to make sure it was working and quickly hung it up when I heard a clear dial tone.

At 4:17 the phone finally rang. I could feel my heart pound as I picked it up. "Hello?"

"Hi, Murphy. Did you make it? Can I come and cheer for you at every game?"

Ashley! I couldn't believe it! "They're going to call any minute, so I can't talk," I said, and I hung up. I guess Ashley was getting used to me hanging up on her, but I didn't care. All I cared about was having a coach call.

At 4:20 Tony walked in. "Well, hotshot, did you make it?" And he slapped me off the head.

I was in no mood. "I'm waiting to find out, creep. And stay off the phone."

As he walked out of the room he said, "Good luck, hotshot. Tell Mom and Dad I won't be home until later."

"Yeah. The later the better," I grumbled, and I settled back to Laurel and Hardy and clock watching.

By 4:45 I started to feel sick to my stomach. By 4:50 I

thought I might cry but realized that would just prove I wasn't ready for Senior League. And as I watched the minute hand tick past 5:15—I had decided to give them an extra fifteen minutes just in case—I took a deep breath, turned off the TV, and started making plans for how hard I would work in Junior League. I'd be a star and show them all. Mom was right—I had lots of time for Senior League.

"Might as well call Peter," I said, talking to myself. "He probably made it. I'll go and watch him play. Like he said, friends no matter what. I'll try to be a good sport about it. I wonder why he hasn't called yet." It was 5:30.

I poured myself a glass of orange juice, held it in my left hand, picked up the receiver with my free hand, and started punching in Peter's number. Suddenly I heard a voice coming from the phone. "Hey, who's on the line? Get off. I'm on the phone."

I put the receiver to my ear. Tony! On the phone! Yelling for me to get off. I hung up and ran up to his room, taking two steps at a time. I slammed through his door and saw him sprawled on his bed, phone under his chin, eating popcorn and talking.

"You're on the phone," I screamed. "You've probably been on for almost an hour." I jumped on top of him and started wrestling with him. "You jerk. I probably had a chance, but you ruined it. They're not going to keep calling. You dummy."

He tried to push me away, but I was so mad I just hung onto him and started punching. I guess I was crying, too, but I didn't care.

26

Dad came running in and pulled me off. "What's going on in here?" he bellowed.

Tony stood up and brushed himself off. "Don't ask me. Ask Murphy. He came in here and jumped me like a little savage for no reason at all." He picked up the phone, listened for a second, and hung it up. "You can ask Amy. I was just minding my own business, talking to her."

Dad was still holding on to me, and I was still crying. But they were mad tears, not baby tears. "He said he was going out. I told him not to use the phone. He knew I was waiting for a call. He did it on purpose."

Dad looked sternly at Tony. "Just how long *were* you on the phone?"

"I don't know. I was going out and remembered I had to call Amy. So I called, and we got to talking. What's the big deal?"

Dad was doing some heavy breathing. He started to say something when the phone rang. One ring—that's all—then it stopped. We all stood there looking at each other.

"Murphy . . . are you up there?" Mom was calling from the bottom of the stairs. "There's someone on the phone for you. Someone named MacDonald. Have you got it?"

"Jerry MacDonald—coach," Dad whispered. Then he hollered down, "He's here, Kathy."

Tony handed me the receiver. "What are you waiting for, hotshot?"

I pressed the phone against my ear. "Yes . . . this is Murphy Darinzo . . . uh-huh . . . okay . . . Monday?

27

Sure thing . . . Oh, and thanks, Coach . . . Sorry you had a tough time getting through.''

Dad looked at me, waiting.

"I made it," I yelled, jumping up and punching my fist in the air. "I'm a new member of Action Lock and Alarm. They're one of the best teams in the league." They also had one of the neatest uniforms in the league— red and white with a small gold lock and key on the front and blue numbers on the back. Absolutely super!

"Good job, hotshot," said Tony. "All that worrying for nothing.'' And he slapped me off the head.

Dad held out his hand and shook mine. "I'm proud of you." And then he hugged me, and I thought we both would start crying.

When the excitement wore down a little, I thought about Peter. I knew why he hadn't called—Tony had been hogging the phone.

I dialed his number and waited. "Hey, Peter," I said when he answered. "What team did you make? You probably tried to call, but my brother . . . What did you say? You didn't? You sure?''

I didn't know what to say. I was so excited I had just assumed Peter had made a team, too.

Then he made me mad. "I'm telling you, I made it by myself. My dad didn't call anyone! Yeah, well, I'll see you around.''

So much for friends no matter what!

Chapter

SIX

Come on, Murphy. The mall is open. Let's go shopping," Mom said as I walked in the door. It was Sunday afternoon, and I'd just finished working out with Dad. "Hurry up and shower so we can go."

"Mom, are you kidding? I hate shopping. Take Kenny."

"Whatever you say. I guess I could buy Kenny new sneakers. But I sort of had you in mind."

"Give me five minutes. I'll be right with you. The Athlete's Foot is having a sale—I saw it in the paper. I know just what I want."

"Okay. But nothing too expensive."

That was the only kind of shopping I enjoyed. At the Athlete's Foot I found the perfect sneakers right off—Air Jumpers, high tops, white with a big red stripe. Mom was a little shocked at the price, but she didn't hesitate. "It's a special occasion, Murphy."

I looked at a rack of warm-ups. "I don't have anything to wear to practice. And look, these are on sale."

She looked at the price tag. "This is a sale? What's wrong with the drawer full of shorts and warm-ups that you always wear?"

"That's the whole problem. I always wear them. They're old. I'm in the big time now. I have to look the part." I pulled out a bright red shiny warm-up with wide blue and white stripes on it. It came with matching shorts and a shirt. "They're my team colors. And they match my new sneakers. What do you say?"

She hesitated a minute and studied me as I held the suit up under my chin. "Oh, what the heck. Take the suit. Dad says you worked hard, and we're proud of you." She picked up a matching gym bag. "Might as well throw this in, too," she said, laughing and taking out her checkbook.

"You're a great mom," I said, giving her a quick hug.

I couldn't wait to show off my new outfit. I put the whole thing on and went into Kenny's room, carrying the matching gym bag.

"What do you think?" I asked, turning all around. "Think I should get Action Lock and Alarm printed on the back?"

"I think you should have *showoff* printed on the back. You're not planning to wear that to practice, are you?"

"Why not?"

"Because you look like you're going to a fashion show, that's why not. No one dresses like that for practice."

"You forget. I'm in the big leagues now."

"I was there once myself, you know."

"Yeah, but that was a long time ago. Believe me, things have changed. A lot."

"Whatever you say, Murphy. It's your funeral."

Dad didn't see my outfit until we were at breakfast Monday morning. He looked at me funny and started to say something, but Mom came in and said, "Doesn't Murphy look wonderful? Just like a pro. It cost me a fortune, but it's worth it. He has to meet his team for the first time today. Doesn't he look great? Show Dad the matching shorts and shirt."

I unzipped my jacket and pulled down my sweats. Dad looked from Mom to me and smiled weakly. "Good luck." I thought I heard him say, "You'll need it," but it must have been my imagination.

Kenny came down with my new gym bag. "I packed a little something in here for good luck, big guy. Take a look when you get to practice. And I packed a towel for you."

"Thanks. I'll be home for dinner, Mom. Practice is right after school." I grabbed my book bag and my new gym bag. At the last minute I grabbed a basketball out of my room. I figured I could practice a little dribbling if I had time.

I dribbled part of the way to Peter's house, but it was getting me too tired. So I tucked the ball under my arm and ran the rest of the way.

Mrs. Patterson answered the door. "Peter left, Murphy. About ten minutes ago. Maybe he thought you weren't coming today. He said something about meeting Michael and Greg."

Why would he think that? We had been walking to school together since first grade.

31

After I put my gym bag and book bag in my locker, I walked into class dribbling the ball. "Hey, Murphy," said Iggy Sands, "I heard you made the Senior League. Show us your stuff."

Ashley, Steffie, Jennifer, Iggy Sands, and Raymond Stubbs gathered around me as I started dribbling behind my back and between my legs. I could tell they were impressed, especially the girls, so I added some fancy footwork to my dribbling.

Peter walked in with Greg and Michael a few minutes later, looked in my direction, and walked into a corner.

I got myself free of my fans and went over to them. "Hi, guys. What's up? How come you didn't wait for me this morning, Peter?"

Peter looked me up and down, checking out my new sneakers, my new warm-ups, my basketball. "You're moving up in the world. Looks to me like you don't need us. You've got your new team."

He sounded so sarcastic that I felt like punching him. But I walked away, found Iggy, Raymond, and the girls, and started putting on a dribbling show again. I knew Peter, Michael, and Greg were watching, so I really jazzed it up.

I was in the middle of a dazzling around-the-body ball-handling drill when the ball slipped out of my hand and rolled toward the door. Mrs. Phister, our teacher, just happened to pick that second to walk in, and the ball smacked her in the legs.

She picked it up and looked at me. "Yours, Murphy? You know the rule. No ball-playing in class. Pick it up after school." And she locked it in her coat closet.

I spent the rest of the day in a fog. I was mad at Peter

because he ignored me. I didn't want to play in gym because I didn't want to get my new suit messed up before practice. And I kept daydreaming about how wonderful life was going to be now that I was on a Senior League team.

When I picked up my ball at the end of the day from Mrs. Phister, she said, "Congratulations, Murphy. I hear you were one of twelve in the city picked for the older basketball group. It's going to be a difficult adjustment, but as long as you keep your good nature, you'll do just fine."

As I left for practice I thought, "What a strange thing to say. Oh, well, what does Mrs. Phister know about basketball?"

_____ Chapter _____

SEVEN

It took me a good fifteen minutes to walk to Westford Middle School, and when I went into the gym, the guys were already on the court warming up. I felt a little lost as I stood in the door, watching, because I didn't know anyone.

A man dressed in old sweat pants and a grubby shirt came over. "You're Murphy Darinzo," he said, shaking my hand. "I'm Coach MacDonald." He turned toward the court, blew his whistle, and hollered, "Come on over. Meet your newest team member." He turned back to me. "That's some outfit, Murphy."

Eight guys jogged over to where the coach and I were standing and surrounded us. They were all wearing very worn shorts and shirts, and sneakers so scuffed and dirty that I couldn't tell what colors they had been when they were new. Each one shook my hand and mumbled "Hi" as we were introduced. I looked like a shiny new penny among a pile of well-worn dollar bills. I felt so out of place I wanted to dig a hole and crawl in.

When the introductions were over, the guys went back to warming up. The coach patted me on the back and said, "Locker room's over there. Change and get ready for practice. You sure don't want to sweat in that spiffy suit."

"Yeah, sure, Coach," I said as I grabbed my gym bag and walked toward the locker room. I was tempted to walk out the door and forget the whole thing, but I didn't have the nerve. Maybe I could spend practice in the locker room—they'd probably never even miss me.

I sat down on a bench with my gym bag in my lap. What was I going to do? I couldn't go out there in my shiny new outfit, but I'd have to. I took off my warm-up top and unzipped my bag to shove it in.

The bag was stuffed full of clothes—old warm-ups, old sneakers, very old shorts, and a top. In the middle of it all was a note that said, "I told you so, big guy. Good luck." It was signed "Ken."

I ripped off my new outfit, rolled it into as small a ball as I could, and stuffed it into my gym bag. I hustled into the grubby clothes and hurried into the gym just as the coach was calling the guys together to start practice.

We started out by doing five laps around the gym, twenty-five pushups and ten minutes of stretching exercises. By the time we started the basketball drills, I was puffing, but I was determined to keep up.

Halfway through practice the coach blew his whistle. "Gather around the basket. Foul-shooting drills. You all know a game can be won or lost on the foul line. Darinzo, I want you up first."

"Me, Coach?"

"Come on, Darinzo. One of the reasons you made this team is because of what I saw you do on the foul line."

He handed me the ball and said, "It's a one-and-one situation. Make the first shot and you get a chance for the second. Everyone gets to the foul line three times."

I was a little nervous, but I had to do well. I wanted to win the team's respect. I took my breaths and my bounces, concentrated on the ball and the hoop, and sank both shots. When I passed the ball to the next guy, whose name was Mo Greene, he muttered under his breath, "Big deal."

I was the only one who made all six shots. The captain of the team, Mark Zabowski (everyone called him "Zabo") was the closest with five. When everyone had shot, Coach MacDonald said, "Okay, Darinzo, once more. Let's see if you've still got it."

I proudly stepped to the line, concentrated, and sank the next two. I felt like one of the team.

The next drill was a two-man offense/defense drill. But each time it was my turn either the defensive man stole the ball or the offensive man faked right past me and laid the ball up and in.

By my third time out I knew I'd have to play cat and mouse. I was on defense, so I spread my arms out wide and crouched down, keeping my eye on the ball. I was going against the co-captain, John Parks, and he must have taken me for granted, because he started to show off. Before he knew what happened, I stole the ball and

drove past him for a layup. I left John Parks standing flatfooted in the middle of the court. The rest of
the team laughed. I strutted a little and laughed, too.

For the next part of practice we played three-on-
three. I wanted to feel like a part of the team, but when
we played offense, no one ever passed to me. I got
boxed out for rebounds and felt quite a few elbows and
knees when the coach wasn't looking. A lot of them
belonged to John Parks.

Then the coach put us into small groups for spot
shooting, saying, "We've got to develop our shooting
skills if we want that city championship." I ended up
with John Parks and Mo Greene.

"Let's see how good a shooter you really are, kid,"
said Mo. "When we spot shoot, we play a game of
P-I-G. Whenever you miss a shot, you get a letter.
First one to miss three is a pig. But I have to warn
you—John Parks here is one of the best shooters on
the team."

I was the last one to try each shot, and I was the first
one to get P-I. I picked up a P when I missed an easy
layup and the I when I clutched on a jump shot. John
seemed to enjoy each miss. Mo complimented John on
each shot he made but never said a word to me, except
when I missed. Both times he said, "Awww, tough
break, kid."

But I was determined. If I lost the contest, I knew I
would lose their respect, too, and I couldn't afford that.
We all had P-I when Mo threw a foul shot and missed.
That left Parks and me.

Parks picked up the ball and went to the foul line. He

pumped it on the floor a few times, looked over at me, and said, "Watch how an expert does it."

The three of us watched as the ball arced high toward the basket, rolled around the rim, and rolled out. Parks didn't say a word, but his eyes got dark and his face got all twisted. Mo let out a low whistle.

I stepped to the line, threw my shot, and won.

Parks glared at me and snarled under his breath, "Don't get too cocky, shrimp. It's not good for your health," and he and Mo walked away.

In the last few minutes of practice, when John Parks came down from a rebound with his elbow in my eye, he said, "You know, squirt, being a hotshot shooter during practice doesn't mean a thing. It's how you handle yourself in a game that's really important." He body-blocked me and sent me sprawling on the floor. "Ya gotta learn to be tough, squirt."

Zabo came over and gave me a hand up. "Don't mind John, kid. He just didn't like the idea of someone your age joining the team. Most of the guys didn't, but John just has a way of showing it more. Don't take it personally—he would have given anyone in your position a hard time."

I guess that made me feel better, but it wasn't going to make my life on the team any easier. Zabo was the only one who even talked to me, and he never called me "Murphy"—just "kid."

As I walked toward the locker room, Parks turned to me and said, "Hey, squirt, where are you going? Pick up the practice balls and put them in the ball bag. Then get the towels and the water bottles. You're the youngest, so you're our ball boy. Tradition, you know." And I thought I had graduated to the big leagues.

Coach MacDonald was sitting in the bleachers, working on some papers on his clipboard. He didn't even notice me as I ran all over the gym, gathering up the balls and shoving them into the big bag. Then I grabbed the towels and plastic water bottles and, feeling like a circus balancing act, headed for the locker room. I guess I could have made two trips, but I was in a rush to get the job over with.

As I hurried through the locker-room door, I tripped over something, and the towels, the bottles, and the bag went flying. I looked up from where I had landed and saw that the something I had tripped over was a cane attached to the hand of an old man.

He shook his cane at me and said, "Better watch where you're going, sonny. You could get hurt flying around like that."

John Parks came rushing over, asking, "Are you hurt? Are you all right?"

I smiled at his concern and said, "Nah, I'm fine. But thanks anyway for asking." I put out my hand to let him help me up.

He glared at me, turned to the old man, and asked, "Grandpa, are you all right? This squirt didn't hurt you, did he? Come on, sit down a minute." He started to take his grandfather by the arm, but the cane came out of nowhere and gave him a sharp rap on the knuckles.

"Don't baby me, Johnny. I may be eighty-two, but I can take care of myself. I can still lick the best of them." He laughed and pointed the cane at me. "But you better help this youngster here. Looks like he's in a mess."

John kicked a towel. "He can help himself. Calls himself a basketball player, but he's not even a decent ball boy. Trips over his own feet."

John's grandfather looked at me. "So you're the new ball boy, eh, sonny? That's a great job for a kid like you."

I started to protest but stopped. If Parks's grandfather was anything like Parks, I'd just be wasting my time.

"Hurry up and get ready, Johnny," his grandfather said. "I'm going out to talk to Coach MacDonald. I'll meet you in the car."

I gathered up all the dropped towels and bottles, then got my own stuff so I could leave. The guys were talking and laughing and joking, and I was pretty much by myself. As they walked out in groups of twos and threes, I suddenly felt lonely. I had always been the center of attention in the Junior League, and now I felt like I didn't have a friend in the world.

Zabo, the team captain, walked by me with John Parks and Mo Greene. "Hey, kid," he said, "you did a good job today. See you Wednesday."

John Parks just threw me a dirty look. Mo looked right through me.

I followed the guys out of the locker room and watched as John climbed into the biggest, oldest car I had ever seen. His grandfather sat high behind the wheel.

Dad was parked behind him in our station wagon, and

as I got in he asked, "Who's that in the old Buick? My father used to drive a car just like that."

I slumped down in the seat. "That's John Parks, the co-captain, and his grandfather. But I don't want to talk about them."

He looked at me for a minute. "Tough practice?"

"Not too bad."

"Are you learning anything?"

"A lot, Dad. I'm learning a lot."

_____ Chapter _____

EIGHT

For the next two weeks I was busy with practice and school. Peter, who had been my best friend for as long as I could remember, didn't have much time for me. He, Greg, and Michael were always together and always busy. Every time I called one of them or tried to make plans in school, they said they were busy. Only Ashley kept calling, but I didn't feel desperate enough to spend time on the phone with her—not yet, anyway.

I called Peter up on a Friday afternoon, two weeks after I had made the team.

"Hi, Peter," I said, and I waited for him to start talking. He didn't, so I did. "How's it going? I don't see much of you and the guys anymore."

"Yeah, well, you're pretty busy all the time with practice and all."

Then it was quiet again.

"What team are you on, Peter? Maybe I could come watch you play sometime." I really meant it. I missed basketball with Peter.

"I'm on Poppa's Pizza. I'm captain this year. But don't come. You'd just be bored."

"No, I wouldn't. Honest. I'd really like to come. You're a great player."

He seemed to like that. At least, it sounded like he did. "Thanks. That's nice of you to say."

"I'm not saying it just to be nice. I really mean it, you know."

Then it was silence again. "Want to come over sometime, Peter? Or go to a movie?"

"I'm pretty busy with the guys on our team. And I figure you've got all those new friends. That team's pretty tight—they go everywhere together."

How could I admit that I didn't fit in? "Yeah. I'm pretty busy, all right. The guys and I get along great. They're a great bunch of guys, you know."

"I've got to go, Murphy. My mom's calling me. See you around." And he hung up. I sat there for a while with the receiver in my hand, trying to decide whether to call him back and tell him the truth. But that would've been impossible.

Dad dropped me off at practice on Saturday morning. "So how has it been going? Are you learning the coach's system? That's very important."

"I'm learning it."

"And you're being a team player? No fancy showoff stuff, right?"

"Right."

"No one appreciates a showoff. Especially not your teammates. You have to be one of the guys, you know."

"I know."

As I walked into the gym I started thinking about

43

what Dad had said. Maybe he was right. Maybe the guys thought I was being a showoff because I was outshooting them. We had had shooting contests at each practice, and even though I didn't win them all the time, I had a better record than anyone else. Maybe that was why they didn't like me.

Coach MacDonald wasn't there yet, and the guys were spot-shooting and playing P-I-G to warm up. I walked over to a group of five that Zabo was shooting with. John Parks was there, too, and so was Mo Greene.

I watched for a few seconds and said, "Hey, guys, can I shoot around with you?"

Parks held the ball and looked at me. "What for, squirt? So you can show us up with your fancy shooting? I told you, there's more to the game than winning P-I-G."

Zabo stood next to Parks. "Let the kid play, Parks. He can't help it if he's a better shooter than you are."

The other guys laughed. Parks handed me the ball. "Tell you what, squirt. You and me will shoot—just the two of us. If I can't beat you, I'll quit the team."

He said it loud enough for everyone in the gym to hear. The rest of the team came over and circled around.

Mo Greene said, "John, if you can't outshoot that punk, we'd all better quit."

That put the pressure on Parks. And on me. We stayed even for the first few rounds, and I could sense Parks getting nervous. Whenever I was shooting, he would prowl around like some caged animal.

"We don't have much more time," Zabo said finally. "Why don't you just shoot fouls until you miss? Whoever gets the most will be the shooting champ." And he said to Parks in a low voice, "Then if you want to quit the team, it's up to you, Parks."

John took the ball and shot first. He made five in a row and missed the sixth.

I stepped up to the foul line and sank the first three by concentrating on the ball and the hoop. When the fourth one went in, I spotted Parks out of the corner of my eye. He was staring at the floor, clenching and unclenching his fists. I took a deep breath, shot, and made number five.

We were tied. All I needed was one more to win. One more and I'd prove that I was the best shot on the team. The big shot. The hotshot. Terrific—then for sure no one would talk to me.

I bounced the ball deliberately, looked up, and concentrated on a spot just to the left of the hoop. I threw. The ball hit the rim and bounced off.

"You're tied," Zabo said. "Let's leave it at that."

"No way, man," said Parks. "We're shooting another round." He took the ball from Mo Greene and went to the foul line. He was taking his time, concentrating hard before each shot, so I went to sit on the bleachers under the basket. I was wondering if my new plan was going to get me accepted when Zabo came over and sat down next to me.

"That was stupid, kid," he said, not looking at me but looking straight ahead, watching Parks shoot.

"What was?" I tried to act like I didn't know what he was talking about.

"Don't blow shots in practice, kid. Not for Parks, not for me, not for anyone. It's a lousy way to try to make friends, and besides, it won't work. Especially not with Parks."

Parks made six in a row this time, strutted off, and stood off to the side, his arms folded.

I stepped up to the foul line and sank six to tie Parks again. I thought a long time as I bounced the ball, took a long look at Zabo, and swished in the seventh.

I went over to say something nice to Parks, but he just looked at me. "I told you, squirt, you're messing with the best! And no hotshot kid is going to outdo me."

Coach MacDonald came into the gym a few minutes later, blew his whistle, and we all sat on the bleachers. I sat behind the rest of the guys and a little to one side.

"Fellows, I have some very bad news for you. I've been on the phone all morning with our sponsor, Action Lock and Alarm." He stopped talking, looking like he didn't quite know how to say what he wanted to say. "They've sponsored this team for the last twelve years." Silence again.

The team started to get restless. "What's up, Coach?" "Yeah, what's going on?" "Come on. Tell us."

"As of twelve noon today Action Lock and Alarm is out of business. And we're out of a sponsor. The league president told me that if we can't come up with a new sponsor by next Saturday—one week from today—we're out as a team."

"What do you mean—out?" Zabo asked. "They can't do that to us, can they?"

The coach slowly shook his head. "I'm afraid they can, Zabo."

"Why can't we play without a sponsor?" Mo Greene asked.

"Because the sponsor puts up all the money we need to operate for the season. That includes paying for uniforms, officials, league fees, trophies, and a banquet at the end of the year."

I finally got up enough nerve to ask a question. "How much does that come to, Coach?"

"Twelve hundred dollars. It's not small potatoes."

A couple of the guys let out a low whistle.

"Well, let's look for a new sponsor," Zabo said. He had played with the team for the past two years. This was his first year as team captain and his last year to play in this league. "We've got a shot at the city championship. We can't let a little thing like not having a sponsor stand in our way."

"I like your attitude, Zabo," Coach MacDonald said. "I'll tell you what. I was ready to pack it in today, call off practice for the rest of the week. But we've still got the week."

"Right," said Mo Greene. "Maybe one of us can find a sponsor."

"If we all work at it," said John Parks. "There's got to be somebody out there who'd want to sponsor a championship team."

Everybody was getting excited and talking at once. The coach blew his whistle and everyone settled down again.

"I don't want to discourage you," he said, "but people aren't exactly knocking down doors to become sponsors. It takes money. And it takes time. And with all the different sports leagues in Westford, there aren't many businesses left who aren't supporting something. I don't even have a clue as to where we should start."

"We'll start at home, Coach," said Zabo. "Listen, guys," he said as he turned to face us. "We can't just give up. We're not a bunch of quitters. We'll all go home and ask our parents and our relatives and our neighbors if anyone knows anybody who wants to bring home a great trophy at the end of the season. If we all pull together, we can do it! Now let's start practice."

We got in a huddle around the coach and put our hand on a ball in the middle. Zabo yelled, "What's the word?"

We shouted, "Hustle."

"Louder."

"HUSTLE."

The third time he yelled, "What do we need?"

"A SPONSOR" echoed off the walls of the gym.

Chapter

NINE

Dad, you'll never believe what happened," I yelled as I rushed through the front door. "Dad, where are you?" I plunked my gym bag down in the front hall and pulled off my sneakers.

Mom was in the kitchen doing dishes. "Where's Dad? It's important. I have to talk to him right now."

She wiped her hands on a kitchen towel, came over to me, and gave me a hug. "What could be so important? You didn't even say hello to me when you walked in."

I gave a quick hug back. "Hello. Now where's Dad?"

"He's in the family room, but he's busy. He's talking to—"

I didn't hear the rest of what she was saying as I headed toward the back of the house to the family room. The door to the room was, for the first time I could remember, closed. But that didn't stop me. I rushed into the room.

Dad was sitting in a chair, talking to a man who was sitting on the couch. They looked up as I came in.

"Dad," I began, panting. "I'm really sorry. But I've got to talk to you right now."

"Murphy," he said, looking stern, "I'm having a very important conversation with Mr. Todenkopf. Where are your manners?"

"I'm sorry. But this can't wait. We lost our sponsor. And unless we can come up with one in a week, our team is out of the league."

"Murphy. I hardly think this is the time." He turned toward the man who was sitting on the couch. "You'll have to excuse my son, Mr. Todenkopf. He gets carried away at times."

I looked closely at the man for the first time. He looked like Humpty Dumpty: big round head, white and bald; no neck; a round body, with hands resting on his belly; thin legs. He wore a flashy red and yellow tie that looked more like a scarf, a pale gray suit, and shiny black shoes. His shirt had a funny pointed collar that stuck straight out.

"Ya, ya. Like mine own son—he, too, gets carried avay." His accent was so thick I could hardly understand him.

"Mr. Todenkopf, I'd like you to meet my son Murphy. He's not always this rude. Murphy, this is Mr. Todenkopf."

"*Ach,* mine pleasure," he said as he stuck out his hand. It was like shaking something made out of warm clay, soft, boneless, and so large my hand almost got lost. He pumped my hand vigorously up and down. I wanted to wipe it on my pants when I was finished, but I figured Dad would kill me, so I shoved it in my pocket instead.

50

"Mr. Todenkopf is here to discuss our community and our school system in Westford. He and his family just moved into town, and the superintendent called and asked me to talk to him."

"That's nice, Dad. But could you just listen to my problem for one minute?"

"Murphy!" He glared at me.

"*Ach du Liebe.* Let the boy talk. Iss interesting to me. Vat iss the problem? I vould like to hear."

Dad took a deep breath and blew it out. "Okay, Murphy. Two minutes. What's the problem?"

I talked as fast as I could. I told him all about what Coach MacDonald had told us. I told him how we wouldn't have a team. I told him how we were all looking for a sponsor before practice next Saturday. By the time I was finished talking I was almost out of breath.

It was Mr. Todenkopf who started talking first. "*Ach.* That iss a problem. Und I can see vhy you are so upset. Mine son—he likes to play the sports, too."

I liked that he was interested in my problem, so to keep him talking I asked, "How old is your son?"

"Mine Heinrich iss eight. He goes into the third grade soon."

"That's really interesting," I said. "Maybe you could bring him over to play sometime."

"Oh, ya, ya. He vould like that. He iss lonely since the move. Mine vife iss still in Germany, settling some last-minute business. She comes in a few months. Heinrich iss not in school yet and hasn't made any new friends."

51

It got quiet for a minute. Mr. Todenkopf was scratching his big chin and muttering, "Hmmmm . . . hmmm." Dad was trying to give me a sign to leave by moving his chin slightly toward the door. I wasn't moving.

Dad finally said, "It truly is a problem, and one we will have to work on. But now I think it's time you left Mr. Todenkopf and me to—"

Mr. Todenkopf put up his big beefy hand to stop Dad. "I think perhaps I haf the answer," he said, and he started nodding his head up and down.

Dad said quickly, "It's not your problem, Mr. Todenkopf. Murphy has taken enough of your time."

He ignored Dad and looked at me. "You need a—how you call it—sponsor?"

"Right—sponsor."

"I am new to this town. I have recently bought a business. A business should take an interest in community affairs. Now—*vie fiel?*" And he stopped talking and looked at me.

"We feel what?" I asked, puzzled. Just when things looked like they might be going well I had lost him.

He chuckled. "Excuse. Excuse. Mine English iss good, but vhen I haf idea, mine mind thinks in German. To be team sponsor—how much?"

Dad spoke before I could. "It's most generous of you to consider this, Mr. Todenkopf, but I don't really think—"

I cut Dad off in a hurry.

"It's twelve hundred dollars, sir. And I know that seems like a lot of money, but we would wear uniforms with the name of your business on it, and you and your family could come to our banquet, and if we win the city trophy, it would go to you to put on display." I talked slowly, hoping he would get it all, but I kept talking. I didn't want to give Dad a chance. He was too polite sometimes and would probably try to talk Mr. Todenkopf out of it.

"Ya . . . ya. Mine family. Heinrich vould enjoy that. If I . . . sponsor . . . vell . . . maybe ve could make—how you call it—a package deal?"

"What do you mean, sir?"

"Vell . . . maybe you could sometimes come to play with Heinrich? Vhile I set up the business? He vould like that."

"Sure," I said quickly. "I'd love to help you out. Like we say in this country, one hand washes the other."

He looked at me strangely. "Heinrich iss a very clean little boy—he bathes . . . oh—you mean ve help each other. Ya, ya. Sometimes I don't catch on to all the American sayings," and he laughed, a big booming laugh. I liked the guy. He had a great sense of humor, and he was willing to shell out twelve hundred dollars to help out the team. Spending some time with his kid would be no big deal.

Dad cleared his throat and said, "Murphy, I don't think you should be so hasty to—"

Mr. Todenkopf put up his big hand again. "Iss settled. Und vhen I make up mine mind, I make up mine mind." He pulled a checkbook out of his inside jacket pocket.

"Twelve hundert, ya? I vill make you out a check. From mine new business. This is *vunderbar!*"

...n't believe it. "Yeah. *Vunderbar*," I said. "Just ... out to Westford Senior Basketball. You have no ...hat this means."

"And neither do you," my dad said to me under his breath. I just ignored him. I knew he was mad that I had interrupted his meeting, but I also knew he'd get over it.

As Mr. Todenkopf handed me the check, he stood up and shook my hand again. I tried to give a good strong shake back. "Und now I must go. This has been a most successful afternoon." He turned and shook hands with Dad. "Mr. Darinzo, you haf a vunderful son. I can't vait for Heinrich to meet him. Come over soon."

"I can't wait," I said. "When should I come over?"

"*Ach*. Ve are still so busy with the unpacking. Ve live upstairs from the business. Perhaps you could come next Saturday?"

"We have our first game next Saturday. How about right after that?"

"*Vunderbar!* Und bring a friend if you want. Heinrich vill be so happy!"

As Dad walked Mr. Todenkopf to the door, I looked at the check. Twelve hundred bucks—just like that. Wait till the team heard! Wait until they found out they would be playing for . . . for . . . what was the name of the business? I looked at the check. *Slumberhaus* was written across it in big fancy letters.

Dad came back into the room shaking his head. "I hope you know what you're doing."

"How can you ask that? It was like he was sent from heaven. What could be bad? Today we lost a sponsor, today we got a sponsor—Slumberhaus."

He just kept looking at me funny.

"So what's Slumberhaus? A mattress company? Beds? Pillows?"

"He owns a funeral home, Murphy. Slumberhaus Funeral Home."

I was nailed to the floor. My knees had turned to jelly. My arms and legs were numb. My scalp felt all tight and prickly. It took a few minutes to get my voice to work. "Slumberhaus *what?*" I squeaked.

"Funeral Home. Slumberhaus Funeral Home."

"You're kidding."

"Why would I kid?"

"Why didn't you tell me?"

"I tried to get you to back off, but you were determined not to let me talk. Besides, I couldn't insult the man's business. He's dead serious about it." He chuckled.

"Dad! This is hardly a time to joke. We can't play for a funeral home. Do you know what the team will do to me? I'll be dead for sure."

"Now who's making jokes?"

"I didn't mean it that way. This is serious. What am I going to do?"

Kenny and Tony walked in to see what all the fuss was about. "What's going on, big guy?" Kenny asked. "We can hear you all over the house. Tragedy?"

I didn't want them to know. I didn't intend to have them start teasing me. But Dad went right ahead and blurted it all out.

"It seems that Murphy found a new sponsor for his basketball team."

55

"So? That should make you a hero," said Tony.

I made a disgusted face and mumbled, "Unless it happens to be a . . . a . . . funeral home." I almost choked on the last two words.

"A what?" asked Ken. "Why are you mumbling?"

"*Funeral home,*" I shouted. "A stupid funeral home."

They both looked at me, then at each other, and started to laugh.

Dad walked between the two of them and put an arm around their shoulders. "It's very serious to Murphy. He's afraid the team won't appreciate playing for a funeral home."

"Do you blame them?" asked Tony. "Would you want to win a trophy for a bunch of stiffs?"

"That's enough," said Dad. "Now let's see if we can all put our heads together and come up with a solution, a way to make the team accept their new sponsor."

"When do you have to have this new sponsor?" asked Ken.

"Next Saturday."

"Does anyone else know who you got?"

"Not yet. Unless you guys tell someone."

"Of course we won't," he said. "The way I see it, if you or one of your team can come up with another sponsor before next Saturday, you can just tell this guy—what's his name?"

"I don't know. Toad something."

"Todenkopf," Dad corrected.

"Yeah, well," continued Kenny, "come up with a sponsor and tell Toad that you're sorry, but someone beat you to getting a sponsor. Tell him maybe next year or something.''

"Kenny," I said, excited, "you're a genius. I'll get on the phone with the Yellow Pages and call every business in town. And who knows, maybe one of the other guys will come up with someone, too. Thanks. And Dad? Thanks for trying to help me out.''

"I didn't do anything. You did it all yourself.''

"You're right. I sure did.''

_____ Chapter _____

TEN

Monday at practice Coach MacDonald asked, "Anyone have any luck yet?"

I looked around, hoping someone would say, "Me, Coach." But no one did. We had practice, but we didn't have our hearts in it.

Every day after school or practice I made calls trying to find a different sponsor, but it was always the same: either a polite "Sorry" or an abrupt "Not interested." Even Ken and Tony made calls for me, so that by the end of the week our fingers must have walked through all the Westford Yellow Pages. A few places had said "Maybe," but they needed a few weeks to let us know, and we didn't have that kind of time. Everyone else was already sponsoring something—youth hockey, baseball, softball, soccer, football, and even badminton.

At the beginning of Friday's practice, Coach MacDonald called the team together. "Well, boys, I guess you didn't have any better luck finding a new sponsor than I did. I know you all tried hard, but I was afraid we wouldn't find anyone. It's a lot of money and it was very short notice."

"What happens now?" asked Zabo. "Can't the league give us an extension? Let us keep trying?"

"No. They made it very clear that tomorrow is the deadline. They don't want any teams playing a league game without a sponsor."

"And what happens to us?" Zabo asked.

"Some of you will probably be able to play on another team. Murphy can go onto a Junior League team. And the rest of you will have to wait until next year and try out again."

A lot of groans. No one wanted to see the team split up.

"And what about you, Coach?" asked Mo Greene. "What happens to you?"

"I guess I'll be sitting in the stands eating peanuts and watching a lot. Maybe one of the other coaches needs an assistant." He sounded sad. "Might as well enjoy what we have left of our time together," he said. "Shoot around. Have some fun. I'll use the office and call the league. After I talk to them I'll let you know what you guys should do to try to get on another team."

As the team straggled onto the court, I followed the coach into the office and closed the door behind me. He had started to dial but hung up when he saw me.

"Coach, I have to talk to you." I was holding Mr. Todenkopf's check folded up in my hand.

"I know you're disappointed, Murphy, but there's nothing I can do about it. You won't have any problem getting onto a Junior League team."

59

"I don't want to play Junior League. I tried so hard to find a new sponsor. I really did."

"I know. They're just not out there."

"Coach, I did find someone. He gave me his check, but—"

"What did you say?"

"I said I found a sponsor, but I have to talk to you about . . ."

He took the check and examined it. "It's good?"

"Yeah, but . . ."

He was so excited he wouldn't let me finish. "Why didn't you tell me sooner? Come on. Let's tell the team."

"No. Wait. Just let me explain something."

But he was already out the door, blowing his whistle and calling the team over.

"Murphy has an announcement to make. A *big* announcement," he said, standing next to me.

When I didn't say anything, he said, "Murphy has found us a sponsor."

The whole team started talking at once.

"You're kidding."

"How?"

"When?"

"Who is it?"

The coach blew his whistle. "Let's let Murphy tell us about it."

I started out hesitantly, feeling embarrassed. "There's this guy. He's new in town. His name is Todenkopf. He wanted to get involved."

"That's great," said Zabo. "What's his business called?"

Might as well get this over with, I thought to myself. "Slumberhaus," I said quietly. "Slumberhaus Funeral Home."

It had gotten so quiet in the gym that I could hear the big vent fans humming overhead. Coach MacDonald was looking at the check. The guys were looking at each other, wide-eyed.

John Parks broke the silence. "Leave it to the squirt to do something dumb. A funeral home? Full of dead people? No, thanks. Not me."

Mo Greene echoed him, "Nope, not me."

A couple of the other guys were saying, "No way. Funeral home? Who wants to play for an undertaker? That's sick."

When Parks said, "Like I said, what can you expect of a ball boy," I finally got mad. I took the check out of Coach MacDonald's hand and waved it in the air.

"Listen, you guys. I know it's not the greatest. That's why I didn't tell you right away. So I made about a hundred other phone calls. But there's no one else."

I slapped the check down on the bench. "Maybe it's dumb, Parks, but at least it was someone. And it's twelve hundred dollars more than you came up with. So why don't you shut your big mouth for a change?"

I turned to leave, then turned around once more. "At least you won't have to worry about having me on your team anymore. You don't have a team." And I walked toward the gym doors.

Before I knew what was happening, Zabo had come up next to me, turned me around, and walked me back. He stood with me in front of the team. "Murphy's right, guys. We *don't* have a team. And no one else came up with a sponsor. So we play for a funeral home. So what could be so bad? We don't have to play *in* the place, just for it."

The team got really quiet, then one kid giggled. "We could *bury* every other team in the league."

Another kid laughed. "Yeah. They'll be *dead* meat."

Pretty soon most of the team was making bad jokes.

"They'll be six feet under."

"Pushing up daisies when we're done with them."

Zabo called for order. "Then it's agreed? We play for . . . what's it called, Murphy?"

"Slumberhaus."

"We play for Slumberhaus Funeral Home."

Most of the team cheered and some of the guys came over and talked to me. Things were looking up. I was feeling pretty special until Parks walked behind me and whispered, "Don't get too cocky, ball boy. You still have to prove yourself in a game."

ELEVEN

On Saturday morning as I started getting ready for my first game, Mom yelled up the stairs, "Murphy, Ashley's on the phone. She says it's important."

I groaned. Ashley was about the last person I wanted to talk to.

"Murphy? Did you hear me? Get the phone."

"Tell her I'm not here," I hollered back. "Tell her I went to China."

When Mom didn't answer, I figured I was safe. Good old Mom. Sometimes I could really count on her.

She appeared at my door all out of breath. "Perhaps you didn't hear me, young man. You have a phone call."

"I told you I don't—"

"And I'm telling you that I will not lie for you. Especially not to Ashley. We're very good friends with the Douglases, and I expect you to be polite to Ashley. Now answer the phone."

I stomped out of the room and clomped down the

stairs. I wanted Mom to know what an inconvenience this was.

I picked up the phone. "What do you want this time?"

"And hi to you, too, Murphy. I'm fine, thank you. So nice of you to ask," she said, pouring out her words like thick syrup.

"Quit it, Ashley. I'm in no mood."

The syrup kept coming. "My, my. Sounds like you have a case of the grumpies. It always helps to talk to a friend. I'm listening."

"Then listen to this. If you don't tell me what you called for, I'm gonna hang up."

Her voice got a little thinner. "I called to remind you that we are 'problem partners' for math, or did you forget? We have two sets of problems to work out together by Monday. Want me to come over this afternoon? Or do you want to come here?"

" 'Problem partners'?"

"You *did* forget!"

I was about to say "Of course I forgot." Anything that had to do with Ashley was instantly forgettable. Instead I said, "I didn't forget. I just had it on hold. We'll have to do them separately. I have a game in a few hours and then I have a job."

"What time is your game?"

"Noon."

"Basketball?"

"Of course."

"You playing?"

"*Of course!*"

"I'll come. We'll do the problems afterwards."

"I told you, Ashley, I have to go to work right after the game."

"What do you mean, work? Chores?"

"No, I mean work—like in a real job."

"Oh, sure."

I knew she thought I was lying, and that made me mad, especially since I wasn't lying to her this time. And before my brain had time to stop my big mouth, I said, "Well, Miss Know-It-All, I *do* have a job. I have to baby-sit for—"

"Baby-sit?" she squealed. "What do you know about baby-sitting? Tell you what. I'll come and give you a hand. I'm an expert. Then we can do our math at the same time."

"Trust me. You don't want to come."

"Oh, but I do. Honest. I'll be a big help to you. And we could split the money."

"Don't do me any favors. Besides, I'm not getting paid. It's for our team sponsor. It's part of a deal I made with him. It's a long story." And not one I wanted to tell Ashley. I felt stupid enough about all this funeral-home business, and I didn't need Ashley to make me feel stupider. "No kidding, Ashley. It's not something you'd enjoy. We can do the problems tomorrow."

But once Ashley got an idea planted in that brain of hers, nothing short of dynamite could get it unstuck. She tried guilt. "That's your whole problem, Mr. Big Shot Murphy. You don't know a good friend when you fall over her. Here I am volunteering my time and talents, and you just want me to beg. Give me one good reason why I wouldn't like it."

"Because I'm baby-sitting at a funeral home." There. It was out. Let her laugh all she wanted.

There was a good five seconds of silence at the other end of the phone. Then she said, "Oh, yeah. Sure! Next you'll be telling me you're sitting for a vampire."

"That's your trouble, Ashley. You don't know when I'm telling you the truth."

"Probably because you never do. Now come up with a better excuse."

"Okay. Enough. You can come. But only because I want to prove to you that I'm not lying."

"Oh, Murphy, it'll be great." Her voice started to get all excited. "We'll have a terrific time, and we'll get all our homework done, and we'll play with the kid, and you don't even have to pay me—"

"Bye, Ashley." She was still talking as I hung up the phone. I'm not really a rude person, but somehow Ashley always brought out the worst in me.

We had a team meeting in the locker room before the first game. Coach MacDonald gave a great pep talk. "We've got the potential to go all the way to the city championships. We've got a great starting five and a strong bench." He flipped through some papers on his clipboard, found the one he wanted, and cleared his throat.

"Those of you who have been on the team know that I play a number system. Your number on the team depends on the amount of hustle and desire you show and how well you play."

I listened as he read the list. I expected Zabo and John Parks would be numbers one and two because they were co-captains. What I didn't expect was to be last man off the bench. But that was me—number nine out of a team of nine.

As we left the locker room, Parks turned around and said to me, "Hey, don't forget the towels and the balls, ball boy."

I dragged out the bag of balls, went back for the towels, and then jogged onto the court to warm up with the rest of the team. I knew the coach was being fair, but last man out and ball boy wasn't part of my dream. I had always been a starter and even a captain in Junior League. But I wasn't going to get discouraged or quit. I'd just have to work harder and work my way up. I'd show them I was as good as the rest of them.

I was wearing an old Action Lock and Alarm uniform because our new uniforms from Slumberhaus wouldn't be ready for a couple of weeks. It was a little faded and wrinkled and didn't exactly fit. The kid who had worn it last year must've been a skinny giant because the waist felt tight but the pants legs came down almost to my knees. I rolled the pants at the waist about five times and wore my shirt out so the lump at my middle wouldn't show. Trouble was, every time I got into the game— which wasn't too often—the pants would come unrolled and sag down to my knees again.

We played a game of four quarters, eight minutes each quarter. There was a league rule that all team members had to play at least one quarter, and that was *exactly* how much time my feet were on the court. I played two minutes at the end of the first and second quarters, and two minutes at the beginning of the third quarter and fourth quarter. I knew I was a great shooter, but I never got a chance to prove it in the game.

I also thought I was a pretty good ball handler, but every time I got the ball I either lost it or got so tied up I had to pass it off. Otherwise I guess I did okay, but it was hard to tell. Just when I was getting warmed up, I'd be put back on the bench. I didn't score any points, but I made some awesome moves without the ball—at least I thought so.

The stands were packed. My whole family had come to the game—Mom, Dad, and even Tony and Ken. They cheered for me whenever I was in, and they cheered for the team when I wasn't. But the loudest fan of all was old Mr. Parks—he sat right behind our bench and hollered and thumped his cane on the bleachers every time the team scored or made a mistake. And whenever John scored, he stood up, waved his cane over his head, and whooped, "Atta boy, Johnny."

We beat Daddy's Deli by ten points, and Coach Mac-Donald gave a quick locker-room talk after the game. "This is a championship team, I can feel it," he said. "I know some of you didn't have too much playing time, but like I said, we play by the numbers, so you all have an equal chance. It's a long season. Hang tough!" I guess he was talking to me, but I wasn't planning on complaining. One thing I was learning: If you want to be a star, you've got to earn it.

After the game Dad put his arm around me and said quietly, "Patience, Murphy. You're the youngest on the team, and you've got a lot of years ahead of you. Just be patient. Meanwhile, work on your ball handling.

You've got to dribble around your man instead of smack into him."

"Right, Dad." My head knew all the answers, but I was still feeling depressed. Last year a star—this year, last man off the bench.

Suddenly Ashley was in front of me, bouncing up and down, shaking a pompon in my face and squealing, "Oh, Murphy, you were wonderful. Simply wonderful. You're *such* a good player."

I tried to figure out if she was being nice or just stupid. Sometimes with Ashley I couldn't tell.

Zabo came over and said, "Hey, kid, we're all going for pizza. Want to come?"

I looked at Ashley, who was still bouncing and squealing, then up at Dad, hoping he'd encourage me to go, but he was slowly shaking his head. "A promise is a promise," he said. "Mr. Todenkopf is counting on you. Ken will give you a ride. I have to hurry—I'm late for my own team practice. I won't be able to come to many more of your games, Murphy. You understand."

"Sure," I answered.

"And do a good job for Mr. Todenkopf. You have lots of time for pizza with the team."

I turned to Zabo, who was still waiting for an answer. "Thanks anyway. I've got to work for Todenkopf this afternoon—my duty to the team, you know. Hey, want to come?"

"Are you kidding? I'm like Parks—you won't catch me dead in there." He started to laugh. "See you at practice, kid."

I turned to Ashley. "Let's go. We've got some serious baby-sitting to do. But don't say I didn't warn you."

Chapter

TWELVE

On the ride to Slumberhaus I sat in the front seat with Ken, and Ashley sat in back. She talked nonstop about how great I was in the game, and Ken kept winking at me and smiling. I slumped way down in the seat.

It wasn't until we were almost there that I realized the funeral home was probably the same one I had almost lost my ball in. Thinking about that creepy place was making me nervous. We might walk in and never get out.

I was about to tell Ken to forget the whole thing when we pulled up in front of Slumberhaus. Ashley let out a little squeal and then got quiet. That made me feel a whole lot braver. "See you later, Ken. Coming, Ashley?" I asked in a cheery voice.

She sat stone still in the back seat, looking at the funeral home. "You're really serious?" she asked in a small voice.

"I tried to tell you. But it's okay if you don't want to

70

come. Ken will drop you home." I slammed the front door.

Ashley opened the back door and jumped out of the car. "Don't be silly. You think just because I'm a girl, I'm a chicken? If you can go in there, so can I, Murphy Darinzo."

"It's your funeral," I said, chuckling at my quick sense of humor. Ashley just punched me in the arm.

Ken drove off, leaving the two of us standing alone, looking at the house. I couldn't believe it was the same place—everything was painted white, cheerful and shining with a new gold sign in front: Slumberhaus Funeral Home.

"We were here before," said Ashley, standing close behind me, "when you lost your ball. But it didn't look like this. It's so big and white. Like a big white ghost."

"Don't be silly. It looks pretty nice, and it's just a house. People live in it."

"Not all of them."

"Huh?"

"Not everybody in there is alive, you know."

Ashley was giving me the creeps. And I was starting to feel stupid standing on the front walk like we were in some kind of trance. I shook my head—hard—and started toward the front door.

"Where are you going?" Ashley asked, still standing where she had gotten out of the car.

I turned around and called over my shoulder, "Babysitting. I'm no chicken." I wasn't sure that was true, but I had to say it if I was going to believe it.

By the time I rang the front doorbell, Ashley was hanging right behind me again.

71

I expected the inside of the house to look dark and spooky, but I was wrong—the inside was as white and bright as the outside. Mr. Todenkopf, looking more like Humpty Dumpty than ever, smiled and nodded as I introduced him to Ashley. She was amazingly quiet.

"Ya, ya, iss so good of you to come," he said. "Heinrich looks so forward to meeting you. He has no friends to play with yet."

"No wonder," Ashley said under her breath. I poked her with an elbow.

"Where is the little fellow?" I asked. And then, talking more to Ashley than to Todenkopf, I grinned and said, "We're both dying to meet him." It was Ashley's turn to give me an elbow.

"I must set up the morgue, und Heinrich iss such an active little boy. He iss alvays underfoot. Iss such a help that you can play with him."

Ashley had suddenly found her voice. "Morgue? What's that?" she asked, fascinated.

"Ach, that iss vhere ve prepare the bodies for the funeral. Vhen they come in ve haf to—"

I cut him off in midsentence. I didn't want to be rude, but I didn't want a lesson in funeral homes. "Just point the way to your kid, Mr. Todenkopf. I'm sure you're really busy, and Ashley and I can't wait to get started."

"Ya, ya," he said, doing his nodding act again. He pointed a fat finger down a long hall on our left. "Heinrich iss in the showroom—through the door at the end of the hall. If you haf problems, gif a call. I vill be in the morgue."

"I'm sure we won't have any problems, sir. We'll be fine."

He disappeared through a door behind him as Ashley and I turned to walk down the hall he had pointed to. But we weren't walking, we were just standing there—again. This was getting silly.

"Go ahead, Ashley. You first."

"What do you mean, me first? You're the one who's got the job."

"Yeah, but you're the expert baby-sitter. Show me what to do."

"We're not baby-sitting yet. We haven't even met the kid yet. You lead the way. Unless you're too scared." And she gave me a shove.

"Who's scared?" I said, marching down the hall, listening to my heart pound in my ears. Ashley was like a shadow right behind me.

"What's a showroom?" she whispered in my ear.

"A what?" I was about to open the door in front of me.

"A showroom. Mr. Toden-whatever-his-name-is said the kid was in the showroom. What's a showroom?"

My hand was still on the big brass doorknob, but I took it off. "I don't know. You go first. You said girls weren't afraid."

"I take it back. What if there's a body or something in there?"

"It's a new business. Todenkopf told my father they weren't officially open yet. There can't be bodies. Ashley, this is silly. Let's just open the door and find the kid. What's the worst that can happen? This place is so white and bright, spooks wouldn't stand a chance."

She just gave me a look and glued herself closer to my back. I slowly turned the knob and pushed the door open an inch. At least it didn't creak.

"What do you see?" Ashley asked in a tiny voice.

"Nothing yet." I pushed the door open just wide enough to stick my head in. I pulled back fast.

"What's the matter?" she squeaked.

"It's dark in there."

"But what's in there?"

"I don't know. But I think I saw a coffin."

"You're just trying to scare me," she said, starting to get mad.

"No, I'm not. You look," I said, and I started to step aside.

As I did, Ashley shoved me into the door, which opened wide. I grabbed her and pushed her into the room ahead of me, saying, "You're the pro. Show me how it's done. Find the kid." But she was like rubber cement, stuck back up against me in no time.

We were just two steps inside the room, and it took us a few minutes to get accustomed to the dim light. It took a few more minutes for us to realize what we were seeing. It was a room twice the size of my living room at home, and it was full of coffins lining each side like new cars. Each was on a tall stand covered by a white skirt, and each had a little sign in front of it. All the lids were propped open except one, a big dark coffin at the far end of the room that had a small spotlight shining on it. It was the only light in the room.

"Murphy, let's get out of here." Ashley sounded like she could barely talk.

"We can't," I said, not quite sure why, but knowing it had something to do with the fact that I had made a promise, and also with the fact that I had Ashley standing next to me. If I ran scared now, she'd manage to make it sound like it was my idea to leave. She could ruin my reputation at school.

That last thought brought back some of my nerve. "Well, well, well, so this is a showroom," I said, trying to keep the quiver out of my voice. "Hey, kid," I called softly. "You here?"

No answer.

"Little Toad," I called a little louder. "Come out, come out, wherever you are."

We heard a faint creak and Ashley jumped. "What's that?" she asked, gripping my arm tight enough to cause lifetime bruises.

"Your imagination." I tried to unstick her.

"Yeah? Well, my imagination is starting to lift the lid on that coffin."

Sure enough, it looked like the lid on the big dark coffin was starting to rise. I was so scared I could hardly breathe. I decided what we needed was more light—things always make a lot more sense when there's a lot of light—so I started looking around for a light switch.

I found a whole bunch of them next to the door behind us, and I started fiddling and fooling around. The first set turned spotlights over the coffins off and on, but that made the place creepier than before.

Then I hit another switch and turned off all the lights by mistake, plunging the room into total darkness. A raspy laugh came from the area of the closed coffin. Ashley grabbed me and screamed—loud—right in my ear. That made me move doubly fast, and as I fumbled with the light switch, the room was suddenly filled with normal light.

But the lid on the dark coffin was now completely open, and we could see something move. Ashley screamed right in my ear again.

"Oh, for crying out loud, Ashley. You want to make me deaf or something?" I pushed her away and started walking toward the newly opened coffin. I guess I should have run, but I didn't want to admit I was as scared as screaming Ashley.

I was almost at the coffin—Ashley had stayed behind—when a low moaning started to come from the coffin. Okay—enough was enough. "Let's get out of here," I said, practically falling over myself.

But Ashley wasn't moving. Her mouth was wide open, and she was pointing at something behind me. I figured she was scared silly. But then she started to giggle. I turned around and looked. There, sitting up in the coffin, was a little kid with the chubbiest round face I had ever seen, munching on a candy bar. He was wearing a big, happy grin.

"It always gets them," he was saying as he climbed out of the coffin. He was dressed in navy blue wool shorts, knee socks, a white shirt, and red suspenders. He brought his pudgy little self over to where we were standing and said in a formal voice, "I'm Heinrich Hermann Todenkopf. You must be the baby-sitters. Welcome." He bowed politely from the waist, adding, "My friends all call me Heiny—rhymes with 'shiny'. You can, too."

THIRTEEN

I was so mad I wanted to kill the kid. But when I looked at his chocolate-covered dimples and his chubby little knees sticking out between the socks and the shorts, I couldn't help laughing. He was half my size and twice as wide. His light brown hair was short and stiff, giving his head the look of a baby porcupine.

"What did you say your name is?" I asked.

"Heinrich. Heinrich Hermann Todenkopf. But I told you before, you can call me Heiny. All my friends do." Then he stopped smiling. "Or else they did. I don't have any friends here."

"Don't you go to school?" Ashley asked.

"Not yet. We just moved here and Papa says we have to wait for some papers. Then I can start. A few weeks." He spoke a little stiffly, but with almost no accent at all, which surprised me.

"You speak pretty good English," I said.

"Mama is English. She taught me. When we knew

we were moving to America, she made me speak English all the time. Papa learned, too."

"Oh. Do you like America? Is your mother coming soon?"

"Papa says in a few months. She is taking care of things in Germany so that Papa could come and get settled."

"Cut the chitchat, Murphy," Ashly interrupted. "Let's get to work on our math problems." She started to take some papers out of a folder.

"Here?" I asked, looking around the room at all the coffins.

"Sure, here. I'm not about to go walking around this house looking for a family room. With my luck, all I'd find is the morgue."

Heinrich had been very quietly unwrapping another candy bar and shoving it in his mouth. He looked up at Ashley and said, "No. No homework with Murphy. He's going to play with me."

"That's what you think, kiddo," said Ashley. "After what you did to us, you're lucky we're even talking to you. Come on, Murphy. Let's get to work."

Before she knew what happened, Heinrich had grabbed the papers she was holding and started to run toward the far end of the room, pumping his chubby arms and legs with amazing speed. Ashley was running right behind him.

"Come back here, you little brat. You're going to smear chocolate all over those papers."

Ashley almost caught up with him, but his short legs were quick. He dodged and weaved around the big open

78

coffin he had climbed out of, and just as Ashley was about to grab the papers he flung them into the open coffin.

Putting his hands on his hips and smiling at Ashley, he said, "Go get them."

"I will not. I'm not touching a coffin. *You* threw them in there, *you* get them out. *Now!*"

"Nope" was all he said.

Ashley was starting to boil. "You listen to me, Heiny." She emphasized the name. "Either you get your fat little heiny into that coffin and get me those papers, or you won't be sitting on that heiny for a week."

He looked at her strangely, but he wouldn't budge. Ashley, totally frustrated, grabbed Heinrich by the tops of his chubby arms and started to shake him. I was about to come to his rescue when he kicked Ashley right in the shin.

"Ouch," she squealed as Heinrich ducked away from her and came over to me.

"Papa said you were here to play with me, Murphy. So let's play."

Ashley, hurt and frustrated, found a chair, dragged it as far away from the coffins as she could, and sat down. "Just get me the math, Murphy. And keep that little monster away from me."

But I wasn't about to go sticking my hand into a coffin either. "Look, Heinrich," I began (there was no way I could call him Heiny). "Get Ashley the homework. We'll play something, but we're not playing hide-in-the-coffin. We'll sit over here and play something quiet."

Heinrich waddled over to the coffin, fished out the papers, and held them out to Ashley, who shot him a dagger look and snatched them out of his hand.

"You owe me one, Murphy," she said, turning her look on me. "A big one."

"You insisted on coming, Ashley. You told me you were the pro when it came to baby-sitting."

She stuck her nose in her book, pretending she hadn't heard me.

Heinrich brought over a board game called Sweet Tooth, plopped down next to me, and said, "This is my favorite game. It is super groovy!"

"Groovy?"

"Groovy! And cold," he said, looking pleased.

"Cold? You mean 'cool'? Where did you ever hear those words?"

"I watch a lot of television in the mornings. Good shows."

I laughed. "No wonder. Reruns. People don't really talk like that, you know."

"They don't?" He looked sad. "I will never be a real American."

"Sure you will. Just don't use corny words like 'groovy' and 'cool'."

" 'Corny'? That sounds like a groovy word. Can I use 'corny'?"

"No. 'Corny' is corny, too. I mean . . . it's . . . oh, never mind. Come on. Let's play."

Heinrich loved playing Sweet Tooth. Every time he landed in the Lollipop Woods or got stuck in the Taffy Trap he'd clap his hands together and shout "groovy,

groovy, groovy." And he kept eating an endless supply of candy that he had stashed in his pockets and all over the room.

Finally Mr. Todenkopf bustled in, all out of breath.

"*Ach.* Iss so nice to see all you kiddies together. Ve do this again."

"Over my dead body," Ashley muttered from her corner.

"Come, come, I gif you a ride home. I haf the new vagon in the front."

Ashley was packed up and ready to go before he finished his sentence. As she walked past Heinrich she patted him on the cheek and said, "It's been a thrill a minute, *Heiny Butt.*"

"I had fun," I said quickly.

"Me, too," said Heinrich, jumping up and down. "It was corny."

I laughed. "Stick to groovy and cool. It makes more sense."

Outside, a shiny white Cadillac hearse with a black top was parked in the driveway.

"You like mine new vagon?" asked Todenkopf as he climbed into the driver's seat.

Ashley looked at the hearse, then at Todenkopf, then at me. "I'll walk," she said.

"It's miles. We'll never make it. Come on. Think of it as a car."

"It's not a car," she whispered. "It's a hearse. Dead people ride in hearses, not me."

Todenkopf had started the engine. "Front or back?" he asked. "Heinrich loves to ride in the back—there's a lot of room for him to play."

"It figures," said Ashley, sounding even more grumpy than usual. She hopped into the front seat between me and Todenkopf and slumped way down in the seat. "I'll just die if anyone sees me," she muttered.

"I love your sense of humor, Ashley." But at this point Ashley wasn't about to find humor in anything, and I vowed that I'd never, ever come back.

When I got home, Mom asked, "How'd it go?"

"Okay."

"Just okay?"

"It was *fine*." She got the message that I didn't want to discuss it, but I knew she'd bring it up again later. As far as I was concerned, I wanted to forget the whole thing. I had done my duty for my team—more than my duty.

Later the phone rang and I could hear Mom talking to someone about me. Since whoever it was seemed to be saying nice things, I hung around to find out who it was.

"That was Mr. Todenkopf, Murphy."

"So?"

"So he told me what a wonderful job you and Ashley did with his son, especially you. In fact, the little boy likes you so much, he wants to know when you're coming back. Mr. Todenkopf would love to have you come whenever you can. He'll even pay you. He said you're the best sitter they ever had."

"Really?" I didn't like the funeral home, but the kid was okay. Besides, I was enjoying the compliment, and the mention of the word 'pay'.

"Really! He said his son is very lonely and wants to

learn to be a real American. Mr. Todenkopf was hoping you could help.''

"Well . . . I don't know . . . maybe—''

"I knew you'd want to help. I told him you'd be happy to. I told him you'd be back.''

"Thanks, Mom. You're a real pal.'' But I knew she had missed my sarcasm.

FOURTEEN

Sunday morning I was lying around the family room watching reruns of cartoons. I kept flipping from channel to channel looking for something new when Mom came in.

"Murphy, what are you doing?"

"Watching TV. Why?"

"But you never watch TV on Sundays. You're always busy."

"Yeah, well, today I'm not busy. Are you going to the mall today? Shopping? Maybe I could come."

She sat down on the couch next to me and put her arm around me. "What's the matter? What's going on? I never see Peter any more. And Greg and Michael don't call. You four boys always spent weekends together. In fact, you were never home. At least, never alone."

"Guess I'm growing up."

"Meaning?"

"Meaning Senior League takes up a lot more time. We practice Mondays, Wednesdays, and Fridays and have games on Saturdays. I don't have much time for my old friends."

"And that's why you're here alone—no time."

"You don't understand. Junior League plays their games on Sundays. In fact, I think their opening game is today. We play on Saturdays. So our schedules don't leave us a whole lot of time to get together like we used to."

"And your new team? Your new friends?"

I didn't have an answer for that one, so I kept quiet and stared at the TV. Mom must have understood what was going on, because she didn't ask a whole lot of questions like she usually would.

She gave me a squeeze. "I did read somewhere in the paper that Junior League games start today at the Westford Elementary gym. Why don't you see when Peter's team is playing and go watch? I think he'd like that. Friends are important. And Peter and you have been friends since kindergarten. It takes a while to make new friends—especially if they're older than you."

Boy, did she have that one right. "Thanks, Mom," I said.

I checked the paper—Poppa's Pizza was playing in half an hour. If I hustled, I could make it. And maybe after the game Peter and I could do something together, like old times.

Mom gave me a ride to the gym. "What time do you want me to pick you up?" she asked.

"I'll get a ride home," I said as I got out of the car.

"Are you sure? It's cold, and you have only that light jacket on. And there's no phone in the gym, so you won't be able to call me."

"Don't worry. I'll get a ride. See you home later."

When I got into the gym, the game had already started. There were no bleachers in the gym, so all the parents and friends were standing behind the sidelines against the wall. I found an empty corner and sat down. Poppa's Pizza was ahead of Plaza Realty 10–2, and it wasn't even the end of the first quarter.

I cheered like crazy every time Peter made a good pass. When he went in for a layup I hollered, "Way to go, Peter" real loud. He looked over and saw me, so I made the thumbs-up sign. He stopped a second, smiled, and gave me the thumbs-up back. He played a great first half, glancing over once in a while to see if I was still there.

Before the second half started, he walked over to the water fountain that was just behind me. "How come you're here, Murphy?"

"I don't know. I wanted to see you play. I guess I kind of miss the league. You're playing a great game."

"Thanks. For coming, I mean." And he jogged back onto the court to warm up.

Poppa's Pizza won easily and Peter was top scorer. At the end of the game I went over to congratulate him and the team. "Nice game, Peter. Congratulations."

"Thanks, Murphy."

"What are you doing after the game?" I asked. "Maybe you could come over to my house. Have lunch with me. Then we could play on the computer. I got some new games. Or we could go bike riding, or—"

"Gee, Murphy, that sounds great, but Coach is taking us out for pizza for lunch. We're going to celebrate. You know how it is," Peter said.

"Oh, yeah. No problem. Sure. I've got stuff to do anyway."

He started to walk away and then came back. "Maybe I could ask the coach if you could come along. Would you like that?"

I almost said yes. I wanted to be included. Then I realized how dumb I'd feel tagging along. I wasn't part of the team or the win. "Nah. Mom's expecting me for lunch, and like I said, I've got stuff to do."

"Maybe next weekend," Peter said. "Maybe Saturday—we don't play on Saturdays."

"But we do," I said. I wondered if he'd come and watch me play. I didn't know if I really wanted him to, but I was about to ask him when one of his teammates called to him.

"I'm coming," he yelled back. He looked at me for a minute and didn't say anything. "Well, one of these days we'll get together again. I have to go, Murphy. The guys are waiting for me."

"You hurry up. I know what it's like to . . ." My voice trailed off as he hurried to meet his team.

I thought about quitting Senior League. Then I could go back on a Junior League team. But that wouldn't be so great either, because those teams were already into their season. I'd be starting late, and everyone would think I was back because I couldn't make it in Senior League.

As I walked out of the gym alone, a cold wind hit me and I shivered a little. I looked around to see if I could get a ride, but I didn't know anyone, so I pulled my collar up, shoved my hands into my pockets, and started the mile walk home.

I kept thinking about practicing extra hard, so hard that the team would realize I deserved to play. Somehow even John Parks would have to learn to put up with me. And maybe someday I'd have friends again—a good friend like Peter used to be.

I was so deep in thought that I hardly noticed the cold wind, and I didn't realize that a car had pulled up next to me until I heard someone say, "Need a ride, sonny? It's awful cold out there."

I looked up and saw John's grandfather in his old car.

"No, thanks," I said. I didn't need charity from the Parks family.

"Come on, get in. Looks to me like you're turning blue. I'll give you a lift home."

The wind rippled my jacket. My ears stung with the cold, and my fingertips tingled. I was colder than I had realized.

"Hurry up, sonny. I don't want to be too late picking up Johnny downtown."

I was too cold to argue. I climbed in, told him where I lived, and held on as he shifted and roared away. Hot air from a vent blasted in my face, and the car smelled like dirty socks, but it was better than freezing.

As we drove, he said, "How come you're on Johnny's team, sonny? Kind of young, aren't you? I thought you were the ball boy when I saw you at practice."

He was making me mad. "My name's not sonny. It's Murphy. And I tried out for the team and made it, same as everyone else."

"No need to get sore. I just saw you had some problems with ball handling in Saturday's game. You'll learn. Just got to work hard, like Johnny does."

I was beginning to think I should have stayed out in the cold.

When I didn't say anything he said, "Johnny's a real good player. Gets his talent from his father. My son John was a great basketball player. Could've made it in the pros, you know."

I thought to myself, "Yeah, sure. That's what they all say." Out loud I said, "This is quite some car." I was anxious to change the subject.

"Some folks think I'm getting too old to drive," he said, "but my reflexes are as good as ever." I held tight as he shifted and squealed around a corner. "This car keeps me young. Don't like to depend on other people to get me around."

He slowed down a little, and he sounded sad as he said, "My son John always wanted to buy me a new car, but I wouldn't let him." Then he mumbled something.

I wanted to ask him what he had said, but I knew he wasn't talking to me. He pulled into my street. "That's my house—the white one." He jerked to a quick stop in front of it. "Thanks for the ride."

"Anytime, sonny. Try to remember it's wintertime when you dress. And try to remember it's basketball you're playing, not football. Go by your man, not into him."

I shut the door and watched as he pulled away. I guess he meant well. At least it was nice of him to give me a ride home. I thought about Parks and his father. I didn't remember ever seeing John's father at a practice or a game—just his grandfather. If his father was such a hotshot basketball player, how come he was never around? Oh, well, that sure was the least of my problems.

Chapter

FIFTEEN

I didn't see Peter at our game on Saturday, but that was okay, since I didn't play much more and didn't score any points. I went out with the guys for pizza after the game, but I didn't feel like I was really part of the team. I felt more like a ball boy tagging along.

At least I made some contribution in our third game. We were up by ten at the beginning of the fourth quarter when I got fouled. I went to the foul line and scored my first two points of the season, feeling really proud when I sank the second shot. I looked around for someone to slap me a high five, but I was being replaced by a sub.

"How come?" I wondered as I walked back to the bench.

"Murphy, you've got to work on that ball handling," Coach MacDonald said. "You should have been around that man and in for a layup. The call could have gone either way."

So much for my two-point contribution to the game.

"Work on your dribbling, Murphy. You'll never move up on the bench until you can get by your man with ease."

I took my place at the end of the bench and watched the team breeze by American Sports for our third win. *Their* third win, really. I wasn't being much help, except for being a first-class ball boy.

After that game Zabo asked me again to join them for pizza, but my heart just wasn't in it. Besides, I had told Mr. Todenkopf I'd spend another afternoon with Heinrich. I didn't have anything better to do anyway. Peter had practice, and even Ashley had made a point of telling me how busy she was when she called me. Heinrich was a lonely kid without any friends, and I was beginning to know what that felt like. Lousy!

Heinrich was in the showroom polishing the coffins when I got there. He was dressed, as usual, in shorts, knee socks, and suspenders.

"Hi, Murphy. Want to help me? These are some of my chores," he said. He was working hard on the coffin he had been hiding in when I had first met him.

"Not really," I answered. I was still not into touching coffins—it seemed unnatural. "I'll watch from over here," I said, and I sat on the floor. I had one of my dad's basketball magazines with me. It had pictures of all the famous college coaches with their teams. I was looking at St. John's and Notre Dame when Heinrich came over and plunked himself down next to me.

"What are you doing?" he asked, peeling open a candy bar and starting to munch.

"Not much. Thinking about how sometimes getting what you want doesn't turn out to be the greatest."

He shoved the last of the candy into his mouth and wiped his hands on the front of his shirt. "I know what you mean. I thought coming to America would be groovy, cool. But it's not. I don't have any friends. Mama won't be here for a few months yet. I'm supposed to start school soon, but I don't want to." He dug into a pocket, opened a box of gumdrops, and offered me some.

"No, thanks," I said. "How come you're always eating candy? It's no good for you, you know."

"Why not?"

"It'll make you fat."

He looked down at himself. "I am fat."

I couldn't argue with that.

"I'm fat. And I'm funny-looking. And all the kids will laugh at me. I will have no friends." He was talking so quietly I could hardly hear him.

"What makes you say that?"

"Because Papa took me to visit the school one day. And the principal brought me into a classroom. And she introduced me." A tear rolled down his round, chocolate cheek. "While Papa and the principal talked, I was supposed to play with the children, but they just laughed at me. I don't want to go back there."

I felt a little sorry for him. "What were you wearing?"

"Like I am now," he said, and I looked at his blue shorts and knee socks, his white shirt and red suspenders.

"And did you tell the kids your name?"

"I told them they could call me Heiny because I wanted them to be my friends. But they just laughed some more."

And I thought I had problems. "Listen, kid. When did you say you had to start school?"

"In a few weeks. But I'm not going."

"You have to go. It's the law. But there's no law that says you have to go looking like that."

"What do you mean?"

"I mean you're going on a program. It'll be a challenge, but I think we can start to shape you up. Want to try?"

"What do I have to do?"

I took the gumdrops out of his hand. "No more candy. And no junk food. Get some exercise. And dress for success."

"I dress like Papa. He is a success," he said, snapping his suspenders.

"I'm talking about American kid-style success. And that means jeans, sweatshirts, and sneakers."

"Just like I see on TV. Groovy!" he said, clapping his pudgy hands together.

"And no more 'groovy'."

He stopped clapping. "Groovy is really wrong?"

"Just old-fashioned. Which reminds me. You'll have to change your name."

"My name? Why?"

"Because you can't go through life being a Heiny. Not in America, at least."

"What's wrong with Heiny?"

"In this country, this is a heiny," I said, slapping myself on the bottom. "And you don't want to be the tail end of everyone's jokes. You get me?"

"Is that why Ashley made fun of me and called me a heiny-butt?" One thing for sure, the kid wasn't stupid. He caught on quick.

"You got it."

"Oh. But that's my name. I can't change my name."

"It's a nickname. And nicknames are changed all the time. Let's look at your name and come up with something snappy. What's the whole thing?"

"Heinrich Hermann Todenkopf."

"That doesn't give us much to work with. Let's see. . . ." I scratched my head, trying to loosen up some great idea. "We could call you H. H.—a lot of kids use initials. Nah—too much of a tongue-twister. What's Heinrich in English?"

"I think it's Henry."

"You want to be called Henry?"

"Not really."

"How about your second name?"

"Hermann." He pronounced it like "Hair-mon."

"Okay, so how about Harry?"

He ran his hand over his short haircut. "Hairy? I don't think so."

We sat quietly a few minutes. I picked up my basketball and tried to twirl it on my finger like I saw the pros do on television. The ball slipped out of my hands and rolled away. Heinrich jumped up to get it. As he gave it back to me he said, "You know what kind of name I'd like? A famous name. A basketball name. How about a name from your magazine?"

I looked at the open magazine and scanned the Notre Dame team. "You just can't pick out any old name. It has to fit you. It has to make sense." Suddenly I stared at the magazine. There it was—right in front of my eyes. I couldn't believe it.

"Heinrich," I said excitedly. "Look at this—the

coach's name. What about his name? He's a famous coach, and it says here that he got his nickname because of his father's occupation."

He picked up the magazine and looked at where my finger pointed. Then he broke into a big smile. "Digger," he said. "Just like a big-time coach. Digger—that's groovy!" He slapped his hand over his mouth. "I mean— that's great!"

"And his father was in the same business your father's in."

"I'm not sure Papa will like it."

"Show him the magazine. Tell him you love Notre Dame. Tell him it's just a nickname. He'll understand, won't he?"

He smiled again. "Papa wants me happy. I'll think of something. From now on I'm Digger."

"Okay, Digger. Let's talk about a shape-up plan. No more candy. Eat fruit instead. Try not to snack. Only three good meals a day. Drink lots of water." As I went through all the right things about diet, I realized how much I had learned from my father. I didn't always follow his advice, but Digger was an example of someone with lousy eating habits.

"Another thing," I continued. "Exercise. Lots of it. What kind of an exercise program would you like?"

"Basketball. You teach me to play basketball. Come on. We'll start now." He reached for my ball and tried to dribble it. When it got away from him, he went chugging after it.

"We can't. It's too cold outside and there's snow on the ground. We'll have to go to a gym sometime. Let's think of something else."

"No. Let's play right here."

I looked around me. "Here? In the showroom? Won't your father get upset?"

"No, he won't. The business isn't open yet. And Papa lets me do anything I want. Come on." He tried to dribble again, but the regulation basketball was too big and clumsy for him.

"You need a smaller ball, Heinrich. I'll try to bring one next time I come."

"Not Heinrich—Digger, remember?"

I got a kick out of the kid. "Right! Digger! But the ball's still too big."

"That's okay. I've got some more balls." He ran excitedly and opened a closet door. It was filled with all kinds of stuff. He poked around and came up with a small basketball.

"Okay, watch." I crouched low and started dribbling. I moved easily with the ball, switching hands, dribbling through my legs and behind my back.

"You're great," he said, and I could hear the awe in his voice.

I stopped dribbling. "I used to think so, too. Lately I'm not so sure."

"What do you mean?"

"I mean the man who's guarding me always stops me cold. Maybe because everyone else is a little bigger than me. It's something I have to work on if I want to play more."

"Let me help you. Show me what to do. You can practice with me."

"Well—I guess it's worth a try." I spent the next few

97

minutes trying to teach Digger to be a guard. But it was no use. He just wasn't big enough and I could easily move past him. It was giving him a good workout—he was all hot and sweaty—but it wasn't doing me much good.

"Forget it," I finally said. "You're just not big enough. I need something bigger than you to try to dribble around."

He stood for a minute deep in thought. "Bigger than me? To dribble around?" He walked away from me and started to wheel the big, dark coffin into the middle of the room. He had snapped the fancy skirt off, and the stand it rested on looked like something you'd put a TV on, only bigger. It rolled easily, even though he could just barely see over it. "Is this big enough?" He stood behind the coffin and moved it easily from side to side. "Let's see you dribble around this, Murphy."

"I have to tell you, I'm not too crazy about coffins."

"So try to dribble by without touching it," he said, and he laughed.

He was pretty good at moving that coffin, and the first few times I tried dribbling around it he moved it right into me. It gave me such a creepy feeling that I was determined to get by untouched. Pretty soon I got better at dodging and faking.

After a while I got into the spirit of things. "This is great. Too bad we can't set up a five-man—I mean five-coffin—pattern."

"Why can't we?" he said.

He snapped the fancy skirts off four more coffins

and wheeled them into the middle of the room, setting them up like five big obstacles close to each other. Then he got his little ball, and I got my big one, and we practiced dribbling in and out and around those coffins.

When Mr. Todenkopf came into the showroom to tell me it was time to go, he laughed at our game. *"Ach,* Murphy. You take such a fine interest in Heiny."

I knew it was time to discuss the new nickname. I told him that Heinrich shouldn't be called Heiny and that he liked the name Digger, and I hoped he wouldn't be insulted.

He seemed to have trouble pronouncing it. It sounded almost like Digger when he said it, but not quite. *"Ach, Dichter.* Iss a fine name. You are a poet now, Heinrich."

"Yes, Papa. A poet. And a basketball player, too."

As we straightened up the coffins, snapping the skirts back into place, I whispered to Digger, "What was all that about? Who's a poet?"

"In German there is no word like 'digger'. Papa thought you said *Dichter,* which sounds almost like it and is the German word for 'poet'. He's happy with the name. And so am I. I will explain it to him later."

When Mr. Todenkopf drove me home in the hearse, we had a long talk about what Digger should do in the next few weeks to get ready for school—how he had to dress, and how he shouldn't stuff his face with candy.

"Ach, Murphy. Iss so good ve met you. You take such an interest in Hein—I mean Dichter." He laughed. "It vill take some getting used to. But you are right. In

America he must be American. Und Dichter iss a fine name."

"That's right. And I'll be happy to work with him."

"Do you haf time? You must haf a lot of your own friends."

"Believe me, Mr. T., I have time."

"Maybe sometime comes the day vhen I can do something special for you, too. Maybe someday you need something only I know about."

I thought about his business. "I doubt it," I said quietly.

"You never know" was his answer.

Chapter

SIXTEEN

Well! Will you look at that!"

"Holy cow! I've never seen anything so black!"

"That's because they're so *shiny*."

"But why the dark purple stripes?"

"They're the colors of death, stupid. Purple and black."

"They're us—the death squad. The other guys don't stand a chance!"

We had been called together by Coach MacDonald for a team meeting an hour before our fourth game. The new uniforms had arrived. They were quite a change from the bright red uniforms we had worn for the first three games.

Across the back of each black shirt, in big fancy gold letters, was written SLUMBERHAUS FUNERAL HOME.

When the team was dressed, Parks said, "Terrific. We look like a bunch of undertakers. All we need is a black hat and a cape. It's depressing." And he gave me a dirty look.

"That's enough, Parks," said the coach. "Let's concentrate on game strategy." Parks hadn't been in top form lately. He had slipped from his number two position on the bench to number three. Sometimes he missed practice, and when he came, he didn't seem to push himself much. It was like his mind was somewhere else. Or maybe he really hated playing for a funeral home. Well, who cared? And who needed him? Maybe, if I was lucky, he'd quit the team.

"The game? No sweat," Parks said. "We won't have any trouble with Pickwick Plumbing." He grinned for a second and then got that dark, cloudy look again. "Unless they laugh us out of the gym." He looked down at his new shirt. "What's this thing on the front?"

I had noticed the emblem as soon as I got my shirt, but I didn't think the other guys had. It looked something like a miniature gold tombstone with our number on it. But it was hard to tell exactly.

The other guys examined their shirts. One kid laughed. "It's your tombstone, Parks. And your number's up if you don't play better than you did in practice."

Parks scowled. "Shut your mouth if you know what's good for you," he said to the kid who had made the remark. "You're all laughing about playing for a guy who works with dead people. But death isn't anything to joke about."

Coach MacDonald broke in. "Enough. We have some business to take care of before the game. Today I'm making two changes in bench positions. Murphy, you move up from number nine to position number seven."

The team all looked at me, and I worked hard to keep from grinning and jumping up and down.

"The next change is in the starting five. Parks, I'm sorry, but I have to move you down to number four."

As Parks muttered something under his breath the coach leaned over to him, patted him on the arm, and said, "Your game's a little off, John. You need to work a little harder and come to practice all the time."

Parks just shrugged the coach's hand away and looked at the floor.

As the team filed out to the gym, Zabo slapped me five and said, "Good going, kid."

"Yeah, good hustle," said another guy. Each team member, including the ones I had moved ahead of, said something encouraging. All but John Parks and his sidekick, Mo Greene.

"It's a long way from starting, ball boy," Parks whispered close to my ear. "And until you can move the ball better, your shooting isn't enough."

Mo Greene just smiled and said, "John's right, of course. You should've stayed in Junior League, where you belong."

Then they walked out. I was so mad I wanted to spit. I couldn't wait to show off my new moves, all the ones I had practiced with the coffins.

"You coming, Murphy?" Coach MacDonald asked from the door.

"Can I ask you something, Coach?"

"Sure, just make it quick."

"Do I really deserve to be moved up? I mean, I know I can shoot, but my moves . . ."

He put his arm around me as we walked into the gym. "I like your spunk. I know it's been hard being the youngest on the team, but that doesn't keep you from working. It's your determination that made me decide to move you up."

"You mean it's not my ability?"

He laughed. "Of course. That, too. Now get out there and play."

I was fired up. Every time I got in the game, I was determined to show everyone that I deserved my new position. In fact, I was *so* determined that I made myself nervous, and I played one of my worst games and almost cost us a win. I couldn't get my feet to work together, and I kept losing the ball.

To make matters even worse, I spotted Peter up in the stands. I had been going to watch all of his games, but I didn't think he knew it. I always stood in a corner and left before his game was over. What a game this was for him to come to.

At least I didn't have to put up with John's grandfather sitting behind us and thumping his cane and hollering at every mistake I made. He hadn't been at the last game, and I hadn't seen him at practices. But that was okay because I sure didn't miss him.

I knew I'd get moved back to the bottom of the lineup. Maybe Mo Greene was right. Maybe I did belong in Junior League.

After the game, in the locker room, the coach called me aside. "You were a little tight today. That's natural after getting moved up. But you're coming. You've got to work on moving better with the ball. Maybe with some of the guys or your other friends."

I took a quick mental count of all my friends and came up with a grand total of two—Digger and Ashley, and even Ashley was back to her snotty self since we had baby-sat together. She didn't call me more than twice a week anymore. And Dad was busy with his own team. Besides, I didn't want to admit to him that I was having problems.

"I want to see some improvement by the next game, Murph. Okay?"

"Right, Coach. I'll work on it."

"And don't forget to get the towels and equipment out of the gym. I'm sorry we have to use you as a ball boy, too, but there's no one else, and you are the youngest."

"Right, Coach." At least I guess he was right—I hated being ball boy.

Just then Todenkopf came into the locker room with Digger right behind him.

"Ach du Liebe!" said Todenkopf, wiping his head with a big red handkerchief. "Such excitement. Such a team. I vill haf a trophy for mine business for sure." The guys just looked at each other as he went around shaking hands with all of them.

"Hey, Digger," I said, "you look great. Come on in and meet the guys." He was wearing jeans, sneakers, and a Celtics sweatshirt. It was a big improvement over the shorts, knee socks, and suspenders.

Zabo came over and, shaking hands with Digger, said, "Hi. What's your name?"

"My name is Heinrich. But my nickname is Digger."

Zabo laughed. "That's great. You play basketball, Digger?"

"Not yet. But someday. I like to come to watch you play. You're a great team."

Everyone smiled at that one except Parks. "Hey, ball boy," he yelled, "did you get those towels and balls out of the gym yet?" He must have been afraid I was getting too much attention.

Digger looked up at me. "What's a ball boy?"

"Someone who takes care of all the equipment during practices and games."

"Wow. What a great job. I wish I could be a ball boy."

I looked at him and smiled. "I have a great idea. How would you like to be the ball boy for this team? You could come to practice and sit on the bench during games."

Digger started jumping up and down, clapping his hands together. "Papa. I'm on the team. I'm a ball boy. Can I do it, Papa? Can I? Can I?"

"Ach, Dichter. You know I cannot say no to you. If it iss all right with the team, iss all right with me."

The guys were all nodding and agreeing—everyone except Parks. "No way. That's your job, Murphy. You're the team scrub."

"Ah, Parks, what's the difference?" asked Zabo. "He's a cute kid. Let him be ball boy. Murphy, show him what to do."

Todenkopf loved the idea of Digger being part of the team. He said, "How about you all come back to mine house und ve celebrate? I haf mine vagon here—enough room for all of you."

"There's nine of us and the coach," Zabo said. "We can't all fit into a station wagon."

Todenkopf laughed. "No. Iss not a regular vagon—iss a . . . how you call it, Murphy?"

"Hearse," I said flatly. "Mr. Todenkopf lives at the funeral home."

The guys all exchanged looks. "Thanks a lot for the invitation, sir," said Zabo, "but we're all pretty busy. Maybe some other time."

"Yeah, we all have a lot of homework and stuff," said Mo Greene.

Somehow Mo didn't strike me as the homework type.

"The team will take a raincheck," Coach MacDonald said. "And by the way, thanks for the uniforms. They came today."

"*Ach du Liebe.* I ordered red, like you had before. But to get that color vould take too long. A company named Remington had ordered these, but they changed their mind at the last minute. All that vas needed vas a new name, und—zippo, you had your new uniforms."

"Figures," muttered Parks. "Leftovers that nobody else wanted."

"They're fine," said Zabo.

Digger, standing next to me, said, "Murphy, can you come over and play with me?"

I thought about the long, empty afternoon ahead of me. "Sure, why not? Can you give me a ride over, Mr. Todenkopf?"

"Of course. First I haf to talk to your coach. I meet you by the vagon."

Zabo looked at me and said, "You're a gutsy kid. You really go over there?"

107

"I think I'll be spending a lot of my free time there."
I figured it would take a lot more dribbling around
coffins to improve my ball handling a little by the next
game.

Digger and I got the stuff out of the gym, then I was
ready to leave. "You coming, Digger?"

"I'll be right there. I'll wait here for Papa. I want to
practice being ball boy." He sat on the floor, took a ball
and a towel, and started polishing the ball, whistling and
sweating over his work.

Chapter

SEVENTEEN

When I walked over to Todenkopf's hearse, Peter was standing next to it, admiring it. I opened the front door, tossed my gym bag in, and slammed it.

Peter kept looking at the hearse. "This is something," he said. "You know the guy who owns it?"

I laughed. "No. I always throw my gym bag into strange hearses." He was too wrapped up in admiring it to appreciate my joke, so I said, "It belongs to Mr. Todenkopf, our team sponsor."

"You ride in it?"

"Sure."

"That's really neat."

We stood there not saying anything for a few seconds. Then, without looking at him, I said, "You came to my game."

He kept staring at the hearse. "You come to all of mine. Why shouldn't I come to yours?"

"I stunk, huh."

He was quiet for a minute. I figured he was trying to find a nice way to agree with me.

"It's a tough league, Murphy. I never realized how much bigger those kids are. You did okay."

"Maybe I should've stayed in Junior League."

"Maybe. I thought I should've made Senior League. I was really mad at you when you made it and I didn't."

"I know."

"My dad found out I just missed making it. Because of my dribbling. They didn't think I could handle the ball well enough to hang with these guys."

"I made it mostly because of my shooting. I'm not doing so well in the ball handling department either."

"I noticed."

"Yeah, well, I'm working on it."

It got quiet again. Then Peter said, "You really get to ride in this thing?"

"All the time."

"Think I could go for a ride sometime? Maybe even today?"

"I thought you had practice."

"It's canceled. I've got the whole afternoon free."

"Peter, I've got a great idea. How would you like to come to the funeral home with me this afternoon? Maybe even work on our ball handling over there?"

"Do I get to ride in the back?"

I laughed. "You are one weird guy. Sure, you can ride in the back."

"Did you say we could work on our ball handling? How can we do that? You got some stiffs that play defense?" He started one of his Dracula chuckles.

"Nope. No bodies. Just a lot of big, empty coffins to

dribble around. By the way, Todenkopf has a little boy who's kind of lonely. I'm trying to help him out. I've got him on a program to get him in shape before he starts school. Help me, okay? Be nice to him."

"Absolutely. Any kid who lives in a funeral home deserves the best. Maybe he'll let me sleep over some night."

"Like I said before, you're one weird kid. But I like you."

"Thanks. Like I always said, you're a good friend. We are friends, aren't we?"

"Absolutely!"

Digger and Peter hit it off right from the start. We all rode in the back of the hearse, and Peter kept pretending he was a corpse. The windows in the back were all covered with maroon velvet curtains, and when we were next to another car, Peter would pop his head between the curtains, put his hands around his throat, widen his eyes, and let his tongue hang out. Digger and I rolled around the floor laughing.

When we got to the showroom, the first thing Peter did was jump into the big black coffin that was Digger's favorite hiding place, cross his arms over his chest, and close his eyes.

"Now I know why Dracula slept in coffins," he said. "Comfortable and cozy. Close the lid, will you, Murphy? I want the full effect."

"I will not. Quit fooling around. We have work to do. Let's get started on the drills."

"You're right," he said as he reluctantly climbed out of the coffin. "All play and no work makes a lousy basketball player. What do we do?"

111

Digger and I got the defensive coffins into position, and the three of us started dribbling. We kept moving the coffins closer together so we'd have to squeeze through tight places. Then we took turns trying to push them into each other like they were big, mean defensive men.

Peter was the one who came up with a terrific bounce-passing drill. One of us would weave to the other side of a coffin and the other one would try bounce-passing the ball under a coffin and up the other side, right into the hands of the other player. At first we kept missing, or the ball would hit the bottom of the coffin and roll away. To be successful the pass had to be sharp and shallow, and we found we could control where it came out on the other side of the coffin if we really concentrated.

It made me feel good to be friends with Peter again, even if it did take something strange to bring us together.

We spent all of the free afternoons we had at Slumber-haus, and by the end of the week, Peter and I were getting better and better at handling the ball, moving in and out of tight spaces, dodging large objects, and passing the ball precisely.

Our next game was against a team who played for the Sock Locker, a sports store in town. They were last year's city champs and had a reputation for being big and mean. As we warmed up, I looked up in the stands to see if I knew anyone. When I saw Peter with Greg and Michael, I got a little nervous. I wanted to play a good game for them. Ashley was there, too, but she always acted like I was a star player.

The game was rough, and two of our starting five fouled out in the first half, so that meant I would be playing most of the second half. I could tell that Coach MacDonald was a little nervous about having me play so much. "They're awfully big, Murphy. Think you can handle them?"

"Trust me, Coach."

Famous last words. When I got in and saw those giants coming at me, I froze. I couldn't get around them, no matter how much I tried. I knew Coach would pull me out of the game. I knew he would drop me back down to last place on the bench.

He called a time out. "Come on, Murphy. Move that ball. Last chance. You can't shoot if you can't get near the basket. Do it!"

Our ball was out of bounds. Mo passed in bounds to Zabo, who passed to Parks, who somehow got himself boxed in by two Sock Locker players. He had no choice but to pass off to me, and from the look on his face I knew he wasn't too happy about it. I started to dribble the ball down the court when I saw a Sock Locker giant coming right at me. I kept thinking, "He's going to steal this ball. He's going to make me look foolish." Then I heard someone from the stands shout, "Think coffins, Murphy. He's no bigger than a coffin. He's a stiff."

It was Peter, and all of a sudden a week of coffin drills came back to me. I studied the guy's moves, faked right, and drove past his left side and in for the layup. When I looked back, I saw him standing flatfooted, looking like he had lost something.

"Nice move, kid," Zabo said, coming over to slap me five with the rest of the guys. Parks just grunted.

I looked up at the stands, and Peter gave me a thumbs-up sign.

I played most of the rest of the game. And even though I had a great game, we lost by two points. Our first loss of the season. It was because of Parks—he played the worst game I had ever seen. Something was wrong with him, but I was feeling too good about myself to worry about his problems.

In the locker room after the game the coach said, "That was a tough loss. I almost thought we had them. Some of you just weren't . . ." His voice trailed off as he looked at Parks. Parks was staring at the floor and didn't look up.

When I was dressed and ready to leave, the coach came up to me and said, "Great game, Murphy. I knew I was right when I picked you. You've got the potential to be a top player. Keep it up. I just wish I knew what's the matter with Parks."

"Maybe his nastiness is giving him a bellyache."

"We need him, Murphy."

"Right, Coach." About as much as we needed poison ivy.

EIGHTEEN

For the next few weeks I spent as much time as I could with Peter and Digger, working on my ball handling. I was getting better and better, but the team was getting worse and worse. We lost two more games, and we barely squeaked by two of the weaker teams.

After eight games our record was five wins and three losses. I had been playing such good ball that I had been moved up to sixth position. But Parks stunk. He had been moved to fifth position, which put him right next to me on the bench. And it seemed to me that since he was playing so badly, Coach should have moved him to the end of the bench and made me a starter.

Parks wasn't being as nasty to me as he usually was, but only because he wasn't around as much. He hardly came to practice anymore, but he was still starting. It didn't seem fair, so during practice one afternoon I got up the nerve to say something.

I was running my feet off during a defensive drill

when I said, "Where's Parks? Doesn't seem right that he doesn't come to practice but still gets to play."

Mo Greene, who was next to me, chose to ignore my comment, so I said it a little louder.

"If Parks doesn't show up, he shouldn't play Saturday. At least he shouldn't start."

Zabo cruised by me during the drill and whispered, "Let it go, kid. I'll explain later."

But when my mouth is on a roll and I'm angry, I don't let go. "No way. It's not fair to the team. Coach said we earn our positions. I'm doing all the work, and Parks still gets the starting position. Not fair!"

Coach MacDonald blew his whistle and said, "Take five. Murphy, I want to see you in the office."

Gladly, I thought. I wanted to get to the bottom of this. I was as good as Parks, and with my hustle and determination I should move into his position. I followed Coach into the office and he closed the door.

He looked at me for a few minutes. Finally he cleared his throat and said, "You've come a long way these last few weeks. I know it hasn't been easy being the youngest kid on the team, and I know there are still times when you feel out of place."

I didn't agree or disagree. I just sat there like a stone, waiting for him to come up with a good reason for the way he was favoring Parks.

"I also know that Parks has given you the hardest time of all. A couple of times I thought about stepping in and talking to him, but you seemed to be able to

116

handle it. I could see you growing up right in front of me.''

I didn't know what to say.

"But I also forgot that you and the rest of the team go to different schools. They're all in middle school, and you're still in elementary, so I guess you don't hang around with them much except for practice and games, right?''

"That's right, Coach.''

"Putting one younger athlete on a team was an experiment the league wanted to try. A couple of the kids who made the other teams have quit already. Maybe it wasn't such a good idea. What do you think?''

"I think I worked hard to make my way up to sixth-man position. But this has nothing to do with my age. It has to do with the team. And practice. And the games. And the fact that if Parks doesn't show up for practice, I should move into his spot.''

He was nodding, and I figured he'd move me up. "Ordinarily I would agree with you. But Parks has some problems.''

"Don't we all?'' I said.

He stopped nodding. "I found out recently that John Parks's grandfather is in the hospital. He's a very old man. He's lived with John and his mother since John's father died a few years ago. John's been spending all his free time at the hospital. That's why he's been having such bad games, and that's also why I haven't dropped him from the starting five.''

Instant guilt trip. I felt like a jerk. Like a heel. No wonder I never saw John's father at practices or games.

And no wonder I hadn't seen his grandfather around lately either.

"Gee, Coach. I don't know what to say. I'm really sorry."

"Most of the guys on the team have been up to the hospital to visit, so I guess I assumed you knew. I wish I could do something. We need Parks. He's a great playmaker. His slump is really hurting us. Without him we don't stand a chance at a winning season, and forget the city championship."

I hated to admit it, but Coach was right—we did need Parks. He didn't like me, and I sure didn't like him, but he made the team sparkle, and we hadn't sparkled in a while.

I just shook my head. "Think it would be all right if I went to see him, too? Parks's grandfather? In the hospital?"

He smiled. "That would be very nice. I think John has a great deal of respect for you. You'll probably end up being good friends."

I let that last remark slide by. I had a lot of names for Parks, but "friend" was not one of them.

"By the way, Murphy, I've noticed a *big* improvement in your ball handling skills. You're getting so you can weave in and around the best defensive man. What have you been doing?"

"Dodging death, Coach."

"Pardon?"

"Just practicing on my own. I've found some big, ugly obstacles to dribble around."

"Well, keep it up. Whatever you're doing, it's

working. Think it's a drill I can incorporate into practice?"

"I don't think so. Somehow I don't think the team would go for it."

"Whatever you say. Just keep up the good work. You've got years ahead of you. Be patient. Keep working. It'll come."

I looked at him and laughed. "You sound just like my father."

He smiled back. "Listen to him. He knows what he's talking about."

After practice Mr. Todenkopf picked Digger and me up. As I got into the hearse I asked, "Could we stop for a minute at the hospital? John Parks's grandfather is sick, and I thought I'd stop in for a minute and say hi."

"Of course. Dichter und I stay here—unless you think I should go with you."

"That's okay. I won't be long." I figured Todenkopf was probably the last guy John's grandfather would want to see.

When I got to Mr. Parks's room, the door was halfway open. I was about to push through it when I heard loud voices arguing inside the room.

"I don't want to talk about it."

"We have to talk about it. I'm an old man. I'm going to die. But I'm not afraid. You have to know that."

"I don't have to know anything except that you're not going to die."

I thought I recognized Parks's voice, except it sounded like he was crying, so I wasn't quite sure.

I recognized his grandfather's voice right off. For a man who was talking about dying, he sounded just as bossy as ever. "John, you have to think about being the man of the family."

I held my breath outside the door, hoping they wouldn't realize I was there. I suppose I should have left, but I stood there and kept listening.

His grandfather spoke. "Please don't cry. I'm not afraid of dying. I'm very old, and I've lived a long, good life. I have some money saved—not a lot, but I want to have a nice funeral. It's important for me."

John was crying so hard he could barely talk. *"No,"* he screamed. "You won't die. And I won't talk about funerals. I won't."

He pulled the door open and ran from the room. He had to push me out of the way to get by, but I don't think he knew I was there. I was standing in the door-way with my mouth open.

John's grandfather looked up at me. "Hi, sonny. What are you doing?"

I took a step into the room. I felt a little embarrassed being there. "I heard you were sick. I heard John spent a lot of time here. I just wanted to say I hope you're feeling better." I turned to leave.

"You heard our argument?"

I turned back, more embarrassed than ever. "I didn't mean to listen. I was just standing outside the door. I didn't hear it all."

I didn't know what else to say, so I asked, "Is there anything I can do? To help, I mean?" It was meant as a polite question, because I knew there was nothing I could do.

He was quiet for a long time. Then he said, "No one can help. No one wants to talk about dying or planning funerals."

I didn't need another problem, especially not one tied up with John Parks. But his grandfather's eyes looked so sad that I said, "I'll see what I can do. I know somebody in the business."

Chapter

NINETEEN

Mr. Todenkopf, I hate to ask, but I need a favor.''
I climbed into the front seat of the hearse.

"*Ach,* Murphy, for you—anything. Look how happy
Dichter iss. I owe you much.''

I glanced through the window behind me into the
back of the hearse where Digger was doing pushups. I
had to smile. He had lost almost ten pounds in the last
few weeks and was looking forward to starting school
soon. He was a great ball boy, and most of the guys
treated him like a little brother. I was really proud of him.

We sat in front of the hospital, and Todenkopf listened closely as I told him about John's grandfather.

"You know, Mr. Todenkopf, I don't like to think
about death. Or talk about it.''

He looked at me for a long time. "Ya. I know. I don't
like death either.''

I laughed. "How can you say that? I mean . . . you're
in the business.''

"This iss a people business, Murphy.''

"Yeah, dead people. No offense." It was a silly conversation, but I couldn't stop.

"A funeral home iss for the living people who are left behind. Young people don't think about death," he said. "Then, vhen they haf to face it, iss hard. Like for your friend John. You tell me he lost his father a few years ago. Now he iss afraid his grandfather dies, too. Iss very, very hard for him."

"But why do people have funerals? They sure don't seem to do much for the guy who's dead."

"Like I said, iss for the living. It brings family und friends together—to help through the hard times."

"It sure sounds complicated."

"Ya, it can be. Iss my job to uncomplicate things. I think, from what you tell me, that John's grandfather worries about John and his mother. I vill go und talk to him."

"That's pretty morbid." I had visions of Mr. Todenkopf measuring Mr. Parks for his coffin.

"Morbid? *Ach,* no. Iss part of life. I vill say nothing to upset him. He talks—I listen. Trust me. I am good at my job. Come. Ve go up now. Just a quick visit. You introduce me."

"Now? Me? What am I going to say? 'Hi, Mr. Parks. I brought you an undertaker. Now you can die.' That's sick!"

"*Ach,* Murphy. There is nothing to be so nervous about. You just introduce me. I vill take care of the rest."

"But what about Digger? They won't let a little kid go upstairs. Maybe you can go tomorrow, by yourself."

"Dichter can vait downstairs. I'm sure they haf books und some toys. He is used to that. Come. Ve go."

123

I had run out of excuses. We got Digger settled into the waiting room working on a puzzle. Then we headed for Mr. Parks's room.

He was watching television on a tiny screen suspended from the ceiling. "Hi again, Mr. Parks," I said. "I brought somebody to meet you, but if this is a bad time . . . I mean, if you're busy . . ."

He picked up a remote control and clicked off the TV. "It's never a bad time to have company," he said. "Can't see much on that ridiculous excuse for a TV anyway. The people all look like ants."

Todenkopf stood beside me, waiting for an introduction. When a few silent seconds passed he cleared his throat.

"Uhh, Mr. Parks, I'd like you to meet Mr. Todenkopf. He's . . . uhh . . . he's a . . ."

"I am team sponsor. Your grandson John plays on the team." He turned to me. "You just vait outside, Murphy. I come soon."

I breathed a sigh of relief. "Sure thing, Mr. T. I'll be right outside if you need me."

I found a chair and sat outside the room. I could hear most of what they said. First a little polite talk about the weather, and then Todenkopf asked, "Und so, how are you feeling?"

"A lot worse than these darn fool young doctors seem to think I am. 'A mild heart attack' is what they say. But I know enough about heart attacks to know that at my age any heart attack means I have one foot in the grave. I'm not afraid to die, you know. That's a natural part of life. I only wish someone would help me plan a way that my death won't be a burden on my family."

"Ach, then iss gut I haf come. First ve plan, then ve pull your foot back out of the grave. I don't think iss time for you to die yet."

And for the next fifteen minutes the two men talked about funerals and heart attacks and young doctors and even basketball. I finally heard Todenkopf say goodbye, and as he was leaving the room, he turned once more and said, "I come again. Ve talk more. Und in the meantime, remember—ve play for the championship in about three veeks. There iss no reason vhy you can't be there."

As we rode down in the elevator he said, "I think he vill be all right. He vorries about his family. I talk more to him."

"Then if he's okay, there's no need to arrange a funeral, right?"

"Not right. That iss the only thing that makes him afraid. But I vill take care of that. Many people make prearrangements—plan their funerals long before they die. I told him, since he iss my first customer, I vill gif him a big discount."

"That's pretty nice of you, Mr. Todenkopf."

"Ya, und maybe John plays better if he iss not so upset about his grandfather. Then I could get championship trophy, no?"

"Yep, you sure could," I answered. Well, I'll be darned, I thought to myself. So even Todenkopf was looking forward to a trophy. I guess everybody likes being a winner.

On Saturday Parks played a super game, and we beat the other team by fourteen points. I played pretty well, too, but with Parks back in top form he got most of the attention.

"Fantastic game, John," said Coach MacDonald. "If we can win the next two games, we're headed for the playoffs."

As I dressed, I listened to Mo Greene ask Parks, "How's your grandfather? Is he still in the hospital?"

"Yeah. I saw him this morning before the game, and he seemed a lot better. He's talking about coming home soon."

"No kidding!"

"Yeah, and he said someone from the team came up to visit him. He said it really helped him out. He was being kind of mysterious about the whole thing, and he wouldn't even tell me who his visitor was. Was it you, Mo?"

When Mo didn't answer right away, Parks said, "I thought so. You're a great guy. I don't know what you said to Grandpa, but thanks. He can't wait to get out of the hospital, and he told me he wants to watch us play in the championships in a couple of weeks. I have to make sure we're in them, and that means we have to win the next two games."

I kept waiting for Mo to tell Parks he wasn't the one who had helped his grandfather, but he never said a word. He just stood there taking all the credit.

I was about to go over and tell Parks the truth, but then I changed my mind. If he found out I had Todenkopf visiting his grandfather, he might not understand. The important thing was that John's grandfather was feeling better, which meant John was playing a whole lot better, which meant we had a better chance at the championship.

The next two weeks flew by. Peter and I spent as much time as we could at Slumberhaus practicing with the coffins. Mr. Todenkopf told me that he had been visiting John's grandfather almost every morning, even after Mr. Parks got out of the hospital. John was at school and Mrs. Parks was at work, so the two men sat around drinking coffee and talking. They had become pretty good friends, but I don't think Parks knew about it.

Actually, I didn't care what Parks knew or didn't know. All I cared about when it came to Parks was that he was playing dynamite basketball. We won our next two games easily, finishing the season with eight wins and three losses. That put us in fourth place in the league and meant we would be playing in the city championships.

The top four teams were scheduled to play in the semifinals the following Saturday. The winners of both of those games would play each other in the finals on Sunday afternoon. And the winner of that game would be city champion.

Our toughest competition would be the Sock Locker. They had finished the season undefeated, putting them into first place, and everyone knew they were already planning their victory celebration. The championship team members would all get jackets, and the sponsor would get a huge gold trophy to put on display. I wasn't sure where Todenkopf would put a trophy, but I sure would've liked a championship jacket.

TWENTY

We rolled by the second-place team—Daddy's Deli—in the first game of the semifinals. We were ready to plan our victory celebration until we sat together through the next game. We watched in awe as the Sock Locker destroyed the third-place team. They beat them by thirty points and, at the end of the game, gathered on the court to chant "We're number one. We're number one." Then the chant changed to "Bury Slumberhaus." They couldn't wait to wipe the floor with us the following day.

On Sunday afternoon we got to the gym an hour before the game, and people were already starting to fill the stands. John's grandfather was in the stands, with Mr. Todenkopf sitting next to him. They were laughing and joking about something. I decided to go over and say hi.

"*Ach,* Murphy. Ve go home mit a trophy today?"

"I sure hope so. But Sock Locker is a pretty fierce team. They're undefeated."

John's grandfather said, "It means nothing. The game's not over until the final buzzer. A lot of worrying ahead of time is just a waste of time—right, Mr. Todenkopf?"

"Ya, Mr. Parks. That iss vat I haf been telling you. Und I am so glad you understand."

"I sure do. I realized it wasn't doing me any good to worry. Just do your best, sonny, and don't waste time worrying." They were both having a great time when John came over.

He looked at the three of us. "Grandpa, you know Mr. Todenkopf? And Murphy?"

"Sure. Sonny and I are old friends, and he came up to visit me while I was in the hospital. He brought Mr. Todenkopf up to meet me. This fine gentleman came almost every morning to visit. We got to be good friends."

"You know what he does for a living?"

"I sure do. That's why I feel so much better. Mr. Todenkopf cleared up a lot of things for me."

"I don't understand," said John.

"I don't really expect you to," said his grandfather. "But I'm planning to live a long time. Mr. Todenkopf reminded me about positive thinking. Now *you* think positive, too, John. And you, too, sonny. We want that trophy," he said, nudging Mr. Todenkopf.

Coach MacDonald came over and told us it was time to get into the locker room. As we walked together, John said, "I don't know what's going on. Right now we have a game to play, but we're going to have a long talk when this game is over."

The stands were packed; everyone in Westford was there to watch the championship game. As we warmed up on the court I saw my whole family, Peter and the guys, and even Ashley and her friends. I said a little prayer—that we would win, that I would play a good game, and that Parks and I could work things out. But I would happily settle for the first two.

We had been warming up a few minutes when the Sock Locker arrived. They strutted into the gym chanting "We're number one," then broke into a jog around the whole court twice, shouting "one . . . one . . . one," each player raising one finger in the air. I guess they were trying to psych themselves up and psych us out. They were doing a pretty good job on me.

The game finally got started, and it looked like the Sock Locker was going kill us. At the end of the first quarter we were down by ten, but we didn't give up. By the end of the half, they were up by only four. I played a little in each quarter and even scored a few points. I think John Parks would have liked to freeze me out, but Zabo wouldn't let him. In the locker room at halftime, Coach MacDonald gave us an intense speech about playing as a team, keeping up the good work, and hanging tough.

At the beginning of the third quarter, two of our starters fouled out, and that meant that, as number six man, I would be a key player for the rest of the game. In the time-out huddle Coach MacDonald said, "With two of our starters on the bench, the rest of you can't afford to make mistakes. I'm counting on you, all of you."

As I took my position on the court, I thought, "Murphy, wouldn't it be something if you could be the hero of this game? Maybe on some amazing shot."

Sock Locker was a tough, hard team, but we played tough, hard ball. We even pulled ahead by one point early in the fourth quarter, but then, with less than a minute to play, we were down again by one. Parks brought the ball downcourt and passed to Mo Greene, who was stopped dead by the defense. Since I was the only man open, Mo passed to me, and I drove in for a layup, thinking about how my shot could win the game. I watched as the ball rolled around the rim, hung there a minute, and rolled out. I followed through for the rebound, but Sock Locker hands snatched the ball in midair, knocking me to the floor.

The ref blew the whistle, and I went to the foul line to shoot a one-and-one.

Zabo patted me on the back and said, "You can do it, Murphy. Sink both of these, and we could win this championship by one point."

I could hear the crowd chanting my name. The ref handed me the ball, and I took three deliberate bounces. I took a deep breath and released my shot; it swished through the net. That tied the score. I thought about being a hero. I thought about my championship jacket. I thought about how Parks would realize I deserved to be on the team. I concentrated on everything except the ball. My second shot was a fraction of an inch short, hit the rim, bounced up high, and was snagged by a Sock Locker player.

Time out was called. As I jogged into the huddle, I knew the coach would take me out. I had blown the shot, and I didn't deserve to be left in the game. "That was a tough one, guys," he said. "Now listen up while

131

we figure what we're going to do in these last thirty seconds. We're not beaten yet.''

As the team went back onto the court I started to take a seat. Coach MacDonald looked at me and said, "What's the matter, Murphy? Quitting? Can't take it?"

"Me, Coach? You mean I'm still in?"

"You're doing a great job. I'm not taking you out just because you missed one shot. Now get in there and play.''

I hustled back onto the court. Sock Locker ball. In-bounds pass. Dribble down the court. Pass to the corner, back to the middle, to the other corner. I looked out of the corner of my eye and saw the pass coming toward the man I was guarding. I put on the steam, cut in front of him, and stole the ball. Six seconds left on the clock, we were down by one, and I had the ball. I steamrolled it up the court, zagging and weaving around Sock Locker players like I was dodging Todenkopf's coffins. I reached the top of the key and heard the crowd shouting "Shoot—shoot." It was a long shot, I knew that. But I also knew that I could probably make it and be a hero. Even if I missed, we'd be tied and go into overtime.

As I got ready to take my shot, a Sock Locker uniform came out of nowhere and crowded me. I could still get the shot off, but I'd be off balance. I glanced toward the basket and saw Parks cutting toward the hole, but there were two Sock Locker uniforms between us, looking bigger than any coffins I had ever played against.

It was a split-second decision. As Parks cut free of his man, I let go with a sharp, shallow bounce pass. The ball skimmed by both Sock Locker players and landed

132

right in Parks's hands. He laid it up and in as the buzzer went off, signaling the end of the game and a victory for Slumberhaus.

The stands went wild. I walked to half court and watched as the team piled on Parks. I stood there watching my dream go down the drain, wondering why I had passed off rather than taking the shot. "What a jerk," I thought as Parks disappeared in a mass of excited players and fans.

Suddenly I saw Parks break out of the crowd and come toward me at half court. The crowd followed him. "Murphy," he shouted over the noise, "that was the greatest pass I ever saw."

"Amazing," said Zabo. "Right into his hands." The whole team was hugging each other and piling on Parks and me, and Coach MacDonald was in the middle of us all saying, "I don't believe it. . . . I don't believe it."

And before I knew what was happening, Parks and I were lifted onto the shoulders of our teammates and carried around the gym.

Parks leaned over to me high above the crowd, all sweating and smiling, and said, "Hey, ball boy . . . I mean Murphy . . . slap me five."

In the locker room we shook up bottles of Coke and poured them over each other's heads, just like the big leaguers do. Mr. Todenkopf came in with Digger, who was holding the championship trophy. *"Ach du Liebe! Und they tell me ve all get jackets. I haf to pick out the colors. You vould all like red?"*

"Are you kidding?" said Zabo. "What color, guys?"

"Black and purple," everyone said. "With a neat little tombstone on the front."

"Tombstone?" Todenkopf looked confused.

"Yeah," said Parks. "Like the one on the front of our uniform."

"Ach, nein. That iss no tombstone. The company that ordered them first—Remington—it iss their symbol. It vass already on the uniforms."

Coach MacDonald looked confused. "Remington? Don't they make typewriters or something?"

"Ach, nein. They manufacture guns. That's a bullet on your uniforms." He looked closely at the symbol on Zabo's uniform. *"Ach du Liebe.* It does look a little like a tombstone!"

We all looked at each other and started to laugh.

"No matter. Iss time to celebrate. I take you all out. My treat. Who needs a ride in mine vagon?"

There was a split second of silence that Parks broke by saying, "Sure. Why not? Me. I'd love to ride in a hearse." And suddenly everyone wanted a ride.

When we went outside to leave, there was a big crowd in the parking lot, standing around the hearse. As we got nearer, the crowd parted and we saw what they had been looking at. Peter and all my old friends had strung big banners around the hearse that said "Slumberhaus is #1." Ashley was tying purple and black balloons to the back bumper.

"I'm going to throw you a big party next Saturday, Murphy," she said. "I'm going to invite everyone in our class to come." She moved forward to throw her arms around me, but I did a quick duck and she missed. I guess that's what Dad meant when he said basketball helps you with life.

Peter said, "Ashley, that's a great idea. We'll all help. What do you think, Murphy?"

I tried to think of a humble answer, but I was too excited, and my voice practically squeaked. "I think that's great!"

The team had piled into the hearse, and Parks called to me. "Hurry up, Murphy. Let's get going. We have some serious celebrating to do."

As I climbed in, I thought about how great life could be. I had old friends and new friends. And pretty soon I would proudly wear a championship jacket—with a tombstone emblem on the front!

About the Author

M. M. RAGZ is the writing coordinator for Stamford High School in Stamford, Connecticut. She literally does her writing on the run, developing story ideas while jogging five miles a day. While her job with the school system keeps her busy teaching writing, conducting writing workshops and seminars, and giving book talks, Mrs. Ragz occupies her free time with a range of activities that includes watercolor painting, crafts, gardening, and summers on Cape Cod in Eastham. She holds three college degrees from the University of Connecticut and Fairfield University. She has traveled to Germany, Mexico, Greece, Britain, and the Caribbean.

She lives in Trumbull, Connecticut, with her husband, Phil, and their youngest son, Michael, who is the inspiration for many of Murphy's adventures. Her other book about Murphy, *Eyeballs for Breakfast,* is available from Minstrel Books.